sting

sting

raymond huber

WALKER BOOKS
AND SUBSIDIARIES
LONDON • BOSTON • SYDNEY • AUCKLAND

First published in 2009
by Walker Books Australia Pty Ltd
Locked Bag 22, Newtown
NSW 2042 Australia
www.walkerbooks.com.au

National Library of Australia
Cataloguing-in-Publication entry:

Huber, Raymond.
Sting / Raymond Huber.
ISBN: 978 1 921150 89 0 (pbk.)
For primary school age.
Subjects: Bees – Juvenile fiction

NZ823.4

Cover image © iStockphoto.com
Typeset in Centaur MT and Myriad italic
Printed and bound in Australia by Griffin Press

10 9 8 7 6 5 4 3 2

For my children,

Jonathan,

Alexandra

and Sophie.

“Life is all one: as big as the world and as small as the honey bee.”

Hattie Ellis

Sweetness and Light:

The Mysterious History of the Honey Bee

CHAPTER 1
Oddbee

"Oddbee," said a Sister as she pushed past me.

I ignored her and kept moving towards the sunlight.

"You're in the way, misfit," said another Sister.

"It's my first flight," I said, but she'd gone. I wasn't going to let their teasing stop me.

I reached the entrance of the hive – thick with bees taking off and landing. When there was a gap in the traffic, I rushed out. The sky was so wide and so blue. I'd stood here before imagining myself flying high and away. Now it was for real. I hovered over the edge.

A sudden gust of wind shot me into the air. I rode on the updraft, racing towards the afternoon sun. The world expanded below me: beehives scattered around the clearing; a rock wall running along one side; and on the other, the humans' track.

Energy surged through my wings and I dived at full speed, pulling up just as my legs brushed the grass. Freedom bubbled inside me. Free of the crowded hive, free to explore on my own at last. But then I saw the Beeline – a highway of hundreds of Sisters flying to and from the field. To avoid it, I returned to the hive. Zabel was waiting for me in the top box as she'd promised she would. She was waxing her legs.

"You didn't tell me it would be fun," I said.

"Fun isn't a word I'd use around the Sisters, if I was you, Ziggy," she said.

"I'm going to check out the field next."

"You know the rules – Brothers don't harvest," Zabel said.

"Why not? There are enough flowers to go around."

Zabel smiled a little. "You always think of a reason, don't you? Look for the hairy blue ones, if you must."

"Hey, you could come too," I said. "Show me that spider web everyone's so scared of."

She looked away. "Some of us have to work. It's my last day in the nursery, thankfully."

"But baby bees are cute, aren't they?"

"Oh, very cute – you feed them all day, then they throw up in your face," Zabel said, straightening the bristles on her head.

I picked a splinter from the box and decided to risk one more question while we were on the topic of babies. "What was I like as a baby? I can't remember."

"That's enough!" she said. "You'll make me batty with your questions. Now finish your training flight – before my Sisters see me helping you."

She polished up the last bit of wax on her back legs.

"Be seeing you," I said, revving my wings and hovering up above the hive.

Zabel did not like questions about when I was a baby. Why was that? Had something happened to me? An accident or sickness maybe. I'd find out somehow. Still, I was lucky to have Zabel around. At least she didn't call me names, not like the other Sisters.

Now I was off to investigate the field – something my Brothers would not dream of doing. When I told Brother Zeppo I was going outside today he'd just groaned and said, "You'll miss the party and it's a waste of your time out there." Then he went back to sleep.

Well, I would prove him wrong.

"Buzz off, Oddbee!"

A bee kicked my backside and I spun sideways. I'd been daydreaming and drifted too close to the Sisters' Beeline.

"Get back in your box, fat boy," yelled the bee.

"No, thanks. Too stuffy inside," I called back, trying to sound cool and unruffled. This name-calling wasn't new – even the youngest Sisters chanted "Zi-ggy the Oddbee" whenever they saw me. But that kick sure hurt.

"You behaving, Ziggy?" An old bee hovered alongside me.

"Yes, Zody. Apart from a sore bum."

"That's what comes of doing your own thing, newbee," she said.

Her eyes darted about. "Don't wander too far. There's a bee wolf on the prowl."

"What kind of bee is that?"

"It's really a type of wasp. A nightmare wasp. It paralyses you, then injects eggs into your body. You remain alive, but when the wolf babies hatch they–"

"Thanks for the advice, Zody," I interrupted. "But I'm sure I will be safe."

She shook her head and flew back home.

Sister Zody was the oldest bee in the hive. She was

always trying to frighten us young bees. "Stick to the rules," she'd say, "or you'll be squished by hailstones, pecked by birds, or torn apart by terror-wasps."

Bee City was behind me now and I flew over the humans' track. It was a black pathway that seemed to stretch almost to the horizon. It was tempting to follow it. I'd seen my first human two days ago, when it came and took honey from our hive. We bees had an agreement with the humans: they gave us a home and we gave them honey. Humans obviously had some intelligence, but where did they live? How did they communicate? So many mysteries to uncover.

Across the track was the field, rippling in a watery heat haze. There was a patch of blue, so I zipped down, landed on a hairy flower and sucked the nectar. My tongue was barely long enough to reach it. The flavour was fruity with a hint of dry grass. *De-lish!* I'd visit the Drone's Club later and tell them about this blue heaven.

Time to visit the rock wall. It was out of bounds, but I figured it should be safe if I memorised the landmarks on the way. I flew over my hive, high above the Beeline Highway.

I'd have to go home soon, back to the teasing. I simply could not work out what I'd done to deserve it.

What did the Sisters see in me? Why did they think I was odd?

As I started flying along the wall, warm air rose from the stones and I practised bouncing from one updraft to another.

The wall went on and on, so I flew up to calculate the distance I'd come. Then a shiver went down my back as I heard a sound like a high-pitched humming.

There it was below me – a flash of yellow.

My body tensed and I powered into the sky. The sound had become a screech and it was following me. Glancing back, I saw my pursuer.

A wasp. My first and it was homing in on its target – ME.

Higher and higher I flew with all my energy, remembering Zabel's lesson about wasps: "They live for two things, to hunt and to kill; and their favourite meat is bee flesh."

Fast thinking was needed. I had two choices: outfly the wasp, or turn and face it. But would the striped assassin listen if I tried to talk to it? No doubt it knew my weakness – that we drone bees have no sting.

Judging by the soundwaves, the wasp was closing in. It was smaller than me, but a faster flyer. Soon it would jab a poison spike into my belly, stinging again and again. Was I imagining it, or did that squealing cry of the wasp form a word: "Dieee!"?

I had no weapon, but surely size was in my favour. Compared to the wasp, I was indeed a "fat boy".

The wasp was obviously in no mood to stop and chat, so I changed course, heading straight for the sun. My eyes could cope with the glare of the sun's rays.

I braked sharply and spun round to face the wasp.

It was coming right at me.

CHAPTER TWO
Wasp

Dazzled by the sun, the wasp smacked head-on into me. The collision sent us spinning apart. My solid body recovered quickly from the impact, while the skinny wasp zigzagged drunkenly down and crash-landed on top of the wall. "Escape time!"

But I couldn't leave. I felt a sharp pang. I'd just hurt another living creature. If the wasp was badly injured, I was partly responsible. It lay on a slab of rock below. I flew down.

Hovering at a respectful distance above the wasp, I called to it, "Excuse me, are you hurt?"

The wasp rubbed its head. A shiny purple bruise was materialising above its eye. "You will die for this!" it squealed.

"Give me a break," I said, "you started it."

"You invaded our airspace. The punishment is death." The wasp struggled to its feet.

"You can't *own* fresh air–"

"In the name of mighty Queen Vespula," the wasp cut in, "you bees will die for this offence!"

What a little hothead. It seemed death and dying were words it loved to use. I tried once more to cool it down.

"Look, I'm sorry we crashed into each other, but you're not bleeding, only bruised. In fact, purple and yellow are complementary colours."

My joke went down like a stone.

"Queen Vespula will hear of this insult," spat the wasp. "You will pay with your life!"

Talking was useless. The wasp was rapidly recovering its senses so I took off. That hadn't gone too well. Despite a thick mop of fuzz that had cushioned the crunch, my head was throbbing. It was the wasp's fault, but I blamed myself for not staying alert. What if it had caught me? I'd be hopeless at leg-to-leg fighting. It was getting late. Time to head back.

I scanned the airspace. What was that moving below? Thistledown drifting past? No. It was a stream of yellow dots flying in and out of the wall. The wasps' nest. And guards were clustered around the entrance.

I shuddered as I imagined what was inside the black tunnel below: a squirming mass of meat-eating wasps. I wiped the picture from my mind. After memorising some landmarks, I headed for home.

The headache began to soften in the evening breeze and I thought about my first big flight: the delicious nectar, riding the wind and arguing with a wasp. Yes, there were dangers out in the world, but I felt more alive than I ever had inside the hive boxes. Now I dreaded facing the Sisters again.

I reached Bee City. The beehive towers threw long shadows across the clearing. I flew into my hive through the entrance in the bottom box and hurried up between the crowded frames. It was slow going but, luckily for me, the Sisters were busy unloading the day's harvest. They ignored me. The hive tower was a stack of five boxes. The Drones' Club met in the top box.

Finally, there they were – my Brothers – snuggled into a warm corner. Most of them were sleeping off a day of feasting. Big Brother Zeppo sat like a king, surrounded by the other drones.

"The party's over, Ziggy," Zeppo said, his snout dripping with honey. "You missed the fun."

"I've been learning about flowers," I said.

"Sissy work," said a tubby old drone.

"Now, now," Zeppo said. "The Sisters keep you very well fed."

I ignored the old drone and spoke to Zeppo.

"And I discovered a wasps' nest. It was pretty creepy. We should keep an eye on them."

Zeppo dipped his antenna in honey. "Not our job," he said.

It was such a Brother comment.

"We could at least help the Sisters keep watch," I said. "It wouldn't hurt."

"It might jolly hurt," Zeppo said, drizzling honey onto his tongue. "This is the sweet life in here. Free food, no work."

My Brothers were unbelievably lazy. No wonder the Sisters got fed up with them.

"Well, I love it outside. There's so much to learn – and not just about flowers."

Zeppo laughed. "You are an oddbee, Ziggy. Sure you're not a bumblebee? They love to waffle on about flowers and peace."

My head still ached from pranging into the wasp and this discussion wasn't helping.

"I don't want to laze around stuffing my face all day," I said.

"Snobby young know-it-all," the old drone said.

"That's a bit thick, old egg," Zeppo said to the drone. "As for you, Ziggy, don't take everything so dashed seriously." He yawned and stretched his front legs over his head.

All at once, a team of clean-up Sisters marched into the Club corner. They began to pick up the Brothers' droppings from the day. I couldn't stomach any more.

I crawled down towards the nursery box. Zabel would be interested in my news.

The gaps between the frames were tight so I sucked my tummy in to avoid damaging the wax honeycomb. Wax was valuable. Zabel said a builder-bee had to eat a day's worth of honey to make just a few flakes of wax.

I passed through the honey-making box. All around me long lines of bees were passing drops of nectar from mouth to mouth. Each bee in the line flicked a tongueful of nectar in and out, in and out. They did it to thicken the droplets into honey but it looked like they were poking their tongues out at me. I watched as the honey was put into cells in the comb where more bees fanned their wings to sweeten it.

Better not linger too long. I kept moving down, past some honeycomb that was being repaired. A group of repair Sisters spotted me.

"Oh my goodness, it's him."

"Oddbee."

"Misfit."

The time had come for me to stick up for myself. I looked them in the eyes.

"Actually, I've been scouting the wasps."

"You mean flouting the rules," said one Sister.

"You'll bring us bad luck, you oddity," said another and flicked a wax spitball at me.

"I am not an oddity! How come you're always so snitchy?"

"It's none of your beeswax," said the spitball Sister.

I'd had enough. I barged through the line and headed down into the nursery box.

Zabel was sitting on an empty comb, grooming herself madly. It looked like she'd been in a fight: wings ruckled and bristles bent.

"Zabel! Are you hurt? What happened?"

"A wasp attacked the nursery," she said.

"How'd it get in?"

"Crack in the storage box. It escaped with a baby." Zabel flattened her leg bristles. "I tried to stop the wasp getting out, but it pushed past me. Ruined my leg wax."

"A wasp chased me too, Zabel. And now I know where their nest is in the wall."

Zabel looked at me and shook her head. "Ziggy,

you have got to control yourself. You broke the rules by going along the wall. I can't protect you if you behave like that."

I didn't tell her that I'd already confessed my wrongdoing to the Sisters.

"But shouldn't we try and stop the wasps? Block up the nest or something?" I said.

"Listen, you're too young to find the nest again. And don't you realise that we honey bees are defenders? We don't go round starting wars."

I spied a pollen grain and popped it in my mouth. "Then I have a better plan. We could talk to the wasps about sharing the airspace."

"You've got a lot to learn," Zabel said. "Wasps are hunters – they always will be. You can't change the world."

My head started throbbing again. Why didn't she want to nut out these problems?

"So you let them break in here and do nothing to stop it happening again?" I said.

"Oh, grow up, Oddbee! You don't know a thing. You're only Day Eight and don't forget it." She turned away and resumed her grooming.

Zabel's words were like a slap on the face. I'd never seen her so upset and it was the first time she'd called me odd. Maybe the old drone had been right and I was being a know-it-all.

"I'm sorry, Zabel. I guess sometimes my mouth runs ahead of my brain."

Zabel paused and looked at me. "And I'm sorry I called you that name."

"Forget it," I said. "So you start your next job tomorrow?"

"Yes, I'm on the royal comb."

"Wow, that's the mainframe of the whole hive. Please, can I visit you? I'd love to meet the Queen."

"Meet the Queen? Ziggy, you know Brothers aren't welcome down there," Zabel said.

I lifted my front legs in the air. "Pretty please?"

Zabel sighed. "I suppose. I'll see what I can arrange. But you may only ask the Queen one question. And you can quit the praying mantis act now."

"Thanks, Zabel."

It took a while to get to sleep that night. I kept thinking about the next day when I might meet the mind of the hive – Queen Zenova.

I had so many questions for the Queen – about the Sisters, my birth, and the humans – although Zabel said I could only ask one.

But would Queen Zenova even talk to me?

Diary of Dr Sophie Domisse – Monday evening

Can't get to sleep.

Probably because I'm reading a book called Safe Handling of Plastic Explosives. *Not the best bedtime story.*

And this army base is a nerve-rattling place.

Anti-terrorist teams are thumping around the training ground – right outside my bedroom.

On the wall above me there's a poster that says, "The Army Wants You!" It points at me wherever I am in the room. Of course they want me – nobody in the world knows more about honey bee intelligence.

I should be happy. The army are paying me to help them with Project Sniffer. It's money that I really need for my own experiments.

So why do I have this sinking feeling?

Something's not right here.

For a start I wasn't thrilled to discover they will be using explosives.

The project sounded fine when the army scientist, Captain Dawkins, told me about it. "Project Sniffer will save many innocent lives," he'd said. "It's a world first for science." That hooked me easily. Am I really that vain?

I've got to keep my head. There's nothing wrong with this job. I'm just here to give them advice on training, and the experiment won't hurt the bees. It's not as if I'm making a secret weapon.

I'll just do my bit and then get back to the experiments with my hybrid bees. I wonder what they're up to right now.

I think I'll read some of Gulliver's Travels *instead – take my mind off explosives. It always helped me get to sleep when Dad read it to me years ago. I still have the old copy.*

Dad wrote this great quote about bees inside the front cover:

"We have rather chose to fill our hives with honey and wax, thus furnishing mankind with the two noblest of things, which are sweetness and light." Jonathan Swift (1704)

It's true – the bees have given me so much. I hope I don't let them down tomorrow.

CHAPTER 3
The Queen

Another wasp was chasing me. This one was a monster – more like a rat than a wasp. We raced over a field of black flowers, but the wasp was too fast. A shadow spread over me, then the wasp latched onto my back and its jaws clacked. I braced for the sting but when it came, the pain was dull.

"Excuse me."

It was only Zody, poking me. Now that I was awake, her antennae felt sharp.

"Sister Zody. I thought you were a flying rat."

"Manners, Ziggy."

"I had this vivid dream about a huge wasp."

"Probably a queen," Zody said. "Did you know there's enough poison inside a queen wasp to kill a thousand bees?"

"Very helpful information, Zody. Why did you wake me?"

"Did I? Oh yes, I have a message. Zabel has arranged for you to see Queen Zenova. I can't imagine how – I've never met her. Go down now. It's Zabel's pollen break. And tidy yourself up." She combed the bristles on my head.

"Thanks, Zody. You're an old sweetie."

I dragged my antennae through the cleaning slots on my legs. When the antennae were polished, I applied some wax to the fuzz on my head – a trick I'd picked up from Zabel.

I felt a tingle of excitement as I climbed down through the boxes towards the Queen. The day looked like it was going to be another scorcher and the hive was in full swing. On the dance floor I sneaked a quick look at a scout, performing a flower dance. The scout circled, waggled and stamped her feet. The dance communicated the exact location, the flavour, and even the number of flowers. Nice moves.

Down I went, through the nursery to the royal frame. There were freshly laid eggs in the cells here. The Queen must be close. Ahead, a cluster of bees was spiralling round a large bee.

"Any trouble getting here?" It was Zabel.

"No sweat. All too busy to hassle me. And I learned a new dance to boot. How's your job going?"

"Easier than the nursery, that's for sure. I'm an attendant: we feed and groom the Queen."

"So will the Queen see me? I can't wait."

"You may not get near her if the Sisters recognise you," said Zabel. "Follow me, and please control your enthusiasm, Ziggy; only speak when you're spoken to."

Zabel eased us into the circle of bees. My heart beat faster. There was constant movement around the Queen. Bees were coming and going with news from the hive. Arresting smells wafted past – the Queen was sending out instruction scents.

The Sisters grumbled when they saw me, and I heard one mutter "Oddbee" again. They began to crowd around to block out the Queen.

A voice cut through: "Stand aside."

The bees parted and there she was – Queen Zenova, sleek and golden, nearly twice the size of a Sister.

"Come closer." The Queen examined my face with her antennae.

"Your question, Ziggy?" she said.

"How do you know my name?"

"Is that your question?"

"No, no. I want to ask about my Sisters. They tease me when I only feel like helping."

"You can't just do as you feel, Ziggy. Each bee must keep in order or the hive will collapse."

"But I've been exploring, and I've learned scouting and dancing. Well, not dancing yet, but–"

Zabel jabbed me from behind and I shut up.

"Come to your question, Ziggy," Zenova said.

I swallowed hard and tried not to sound so nervous. "Why do they call me Oddbee?"

The Queen paused for a moment, then said, "There are thousands of different bees in the world. It's time you met some of them."

"Where do they live, Queen Zenova?"

"Follow the rock wall, past the wasps' nest to the end."

So she knew about the wasps already.

"Shouldn't we do something about them – the wasps, I mean? Ow!" Zabel kicked me this time.

"Don't worry, we'll protect the hive," Zenova said.

"The truth is, I sort of bumped into a wasp yesterday and it seemed pretty angry."

"They all are. The wasp Queen, Vespula, has threatened me many times. Now go, Ziggy, I have a beehive to run."

"Thank you, Queen Zenova," I said.

The Queen kindly extended Zabel's break and we walked down to the entrance at the bottom of the hive. The guards were trying to get rid of a cicada that was stuck on its back. The stupid thing was tizzying around in circles while they tried to flip it over. If the bug blundered inside, one of the Sisters might have to sting it. Zabel had explained the risks of stinging. A bee usually died when it stung larger creatures.

"Queen Zenova told us how a mouse died inside the hive during the big snow," said Zabel. "It was too heavy to drag out so they mummified it in bee-putty."

"What's beyond the rock wall?"

"The scouts say it's a no-go zone," she said. "I can't understand why Zenova is sending you there. A young bee could get lost."

"So do you think I should go?"

"Well, Ziggy, it's not every day the Queen commands someone to break the rules. I suppose she picked the best bee to do that."

"Thanks, Zabel. Maybe we could search for that mouse-mummy when I return."

"Forget it. I don't have time to play – there's too much work to do."

Beside us the cicada had been righted and was now fizzing in irritation as it crawled into the grass. I revved my wings.

"Be seeing you, Zabel," I said, and set off.

Flying high above the rock wall, I kept an eye out for wasp scouts. The wall was long and my thoughts turned to Queen Zenova. I'd been so tongue-tied with her. She hadn't actually answered my question about being an oddbee. Instead, she'd sent me into a forbidden zone. It seemed crazy but at least I was out of the hive again.

I saw the end of the rocks ahead and rising up in front of me was a wall of greenery. A forest. A wild place from one of Zody's stories: "Let me tell you the story about the bee who was trapped by a forest spider." Thank you for that one, Zody. I gathered my courage and winged between the trees.

It was a hot day but the air was refreshing. Shafts of sunlight lit the forest floor. The pools of light attracted a myriad of flying creatures. A sparkle drew me towards a fallen tree. The black bark appeared to be covered in droplets of honey. As I flew closer, I noticed tiny bugs were feeding on the tree. It looked like the bugs were excreting the glistening drops from their rear ends. I landed and examined the liquid. It smelled like honey so I dipped a foot into a droplet. It tasted like honey too – not bad for a bug's dropping! This honeydew would do for breakfast. I began slurping the sweet syrup. It was much easier than trying to get my short tongue inside a flower to drink. As I drank, I realised that the forest had become hushed around me. Even the humming of the flies had stopped.

Everything was still for a moment. Then I heard a fluttering sound. A shadow danced across the log. It was a bird and it was about to land on top of me.

I froze.

CHAPTER FOUR

Wild Bee

The bird landed on the log beside me. It tilted its head to one side. A dark eye looked me over. Was I just a snack to him? I reckoned that in a chase I could probably fly faster than the bird. But maybe I'd have a better chance if I stayed still and played dead bee.

The bird made up its mind. It thrust its beak into the bark beside me. *Tock, tock, tock.* It was eating the bugs that made the honeydew.

"Cut it out, Flitt," said a voice overhead.

A small bee was circling above us. The bird squawked.

"I know you're hungry," said the bee, "but you'll give my friend here a heart attack."

The bird took off and flew in jerky circles away into the trees.

"Don't worry about Flitt," said the bee, settling next to me on the log. "He's just fooling with you."

"Well, it worked. I feel like a bit of a twit," I said.

The bee laughed. "My name's Xola."

"Mine's Ziggy – as in piggy. And if I hadn't been pigging out on honeydew, I might've spied that bird sooner. Is Flitt your friend?"

"Let's just say he's not my enemy," Xola said. "We've got a deal. He doesn't bother me and I tell him where the juiciest sandflies are hanging out."

This bee was so different. She had a dark, compact body and shiny black eyes. Her back legs had small pouches for collecting pollen.

"Which hive are you from?" I asked.

"I don't come from a hive, dopey. I'm a wild bee."

"But how do you live without the humans' boxes?" I asked.

"Humans! Ugly creatures – don't need 'em. The forest gives us a home."

"What about predators?"

"So many questions from so young a bee. Come on, I'll show you where the gang lives."

Xola took off. Who was the "gang"? And could I trust this little bee? I couldn't know for sure, but there was something about Xola that put me at ease. I flew after her.

So here I was, just turned Day Nine, in a dangerous forest, and following a stranger. Maybe I *was* a bit loopy.

Xola was a snappy flyer. She could dodge branches, skim streams and dive into gullies, all without hesitating. Either she knows this forest well or she's mad, I thought, as I tried to avoid trees that came rushing at me.

At last, we arrived at a clearing. There was only one tree here: a gnarly old thing. The ground around it was pocked with hundreds of holes. Each hole had a crater of soil built up at its entrance. Wild bees were flying in and out.

Xola dropped into a hole but I hovered above – unsure. What would Zabel say about all this? Curiosity led me on. I crawled into a tunnel which opened out into a small chamber carved out of clay. The floor was littered with food scraps.

"Welcome to my place," announced Xola.

I pictured the thousands of bees I shared a room with at home. "You live here alone – all by yourself?"

"Yep, that's what alone means. Excuse the mess."

"We have clean-up bees in our hive," I said. I looked at the crumbling walls, the scraps, the odd tree root poking through. "Your home is ... *interesting*."

"When someone says interesting, it usually means 'weird'," Xola said.

"Oh, I didn't mean to be rude." I scratched my head with my back leg. "It's just that we honey bees have stricter rules about keeping house. Where's your queen?"

"Don't believe in 'em."

"No queen?" I could hardly believe what I was hearing. "So who's in charge?"

"No one. We do our own thing. My friend Xena lives nearby if I need help. But who is looking after you, Ziggy? There's a wee mystery. What's a baby-faced drone doing in the wilderness?"

What a cheeky thing she is, I thought. "I am here at Queen Zenova's command," I said. "To see how other bees live. The truth is, I don't fit in at home. I'm not like my Brothers."

"I don't get it. You drones have a soft life," said Xola.

"We do, but it just doesn't appeal to me. I'd prefer to work."

"A working drone – now *that's* interesting. Can you dance too? I hear you honey bees really melt the wax."

"I haven't learned to dance yet," I admitted. My face got all hot and I nervously scratched the wall with my antenna. A chunk of clay fell off.

"Oops. You know, I wouldn't mind living here, Xola. No pesky rules, freedom to fly anywhere, anytime."

"You'd miss the crowds, Ziggy. And the forest is no playground. The honeydew attracts some wicked wasps."

Wasps. The word expanded to fill my mind. A shadow passed over my eyes.

"Are you okay?" Xola asked. "You look spaced out."

"Something just happened in my head. I can't explain it."

"Did I scare you with my talk of wasps?"

Wasps. A shiver went down my back and I pressed my head against the wall.

"It reminds me of my dream this morning but this time I'm awake. Maybe it's a warning."

"Or a message from the hive," Xola said. "Calling Ziggy, the mystery bee." She smiled.

"Seriously, I'm worried," I said. "I should go home now. They might need me."

"I'll fly back with you."

"Are you sure?" I asked.

"How could I resist a chance to visit the clean, strictly organised Bee City? Come on – what are we waiting for?"

Xola led the way back to the forest edge. Once we reached the wall I took over the lead. I flew with all my energy and I think even zippy Xola had trouble keeping up. We slowed down at the wasps' nest. There was very little activity around the entrance. Where were all the wasps?

"Only three guards," I said. "Doesn't seem right."

"You can count them from this high up?"

"Yeah. We drones have ten thousand lenses in each eye."

"Is that how you spend all those lazy days – counting lenses?"

"No, it's commonly known that . . ." I noticed Xola grinning. "Hey, you're pulling my leg again."

"Just tell me about the wasps, Ziggy."

"They hate bees," I said. "I wish I knew why."

I told Xola about my collision with the death-talking wasp and its promise to punish the hive for my blunder.

"What worries me is that the wasp Queen, Vespula, may use it as an excuse to destroy my hive."

We were approaching Bee City at last.

Then I saw it: a dark cloud on the far side of the clearing. My head started thumping.

The air was alive with wasps. Directly over my hive.

CHAPTER FIVE
Terror

My worst fear was coming true. As we flew closer, it became clear there was a fierce battle raging.

A war between bees and wasps.

"Your alarm sense was right, Ziggy. The wasps are probably after your honey."

"No, it's all my fault."

"Rubbish," Xola said. "Wasps love a spot of robbery."

We positioned ourselves high above the hive. It seemed the bees were struggling to repel the wasps.

"It's hardly a fair fight," I said. "Wasps can sting more than bees."

"Why's that?"

"Zabel said that bees' stingers have hooks on them, so they get stuck easily. Wasps have smooth stings."

"They are evil beasties," Xola said.

"Look, they're targeting the entrance now."

I watched, sickened to see a wasp intercept a Sister who had just taken off. The wasp gripped onto the back of the bee and together they tumbled through the air. A moment before hitting the ground, the wasp released the wounded bee from its deadly embrace. I felt helpless.

"They hit the bees just after take-off," Xola explained. "Your Sisters should tackle the wasps on the ground."

"You're right. Maybe it's not so hopeless. A grounded wasp isn't as dangerous."

I saw a wasp land at the hive entrance and crawl inside. It came rolling back out in a flash, pursued by two guards. They kicked the wasp with their hind legs and it was hurled into the long grass.

Further up the stack of hive boxes, a flurry of wasps was trying to get in through a crack.

"I've gotta do something," I said. "It's a feeding frenzy."

"What can you do? They're born killers," Xola said.

Somewhere down there in the battle arena was dear Zabel.

"I must find my Sister. We can't let the wasps frighten us."

"Let's not muck around then. You take the front

door, I'll go for the cracked box," Xola said.

She was off. Wild bees didn't wait to discuss things. It was now or never for me too. I dropped towards the hive. The airspace was filled with sound: the war cry of wasps and the buzzing of bees.

A wasp tried to land on top of me, but my eyes were scanning all around and I saw it coming. I twisted my abdomen and it failed to get a grip on me. Then a large bee plummeted past with a wasp already clinging to its back. I had to knock that wasp off before it was too late. When it saw me zooming towards it, the wasp released the bee. The bee fell into the grass.

It was then that I saw who it was; Brother Zeppo lay lifeless on his back. He must've come out to help defend the hive. I landed beside him in the dry grass. My stomach turned. Only yesterday I'd criticised Zeppo for being lazy, but here he was trying to chase off the wasps. And now he was dead. Poor Zeppo. He was the gentlest bee I knew.

I had to find Zabel.

My wings had just reached take-off speed, when Zeppo's body twitched. He was still alive! I carefully rolled him over.

"Zeppo! Can you hear me, Brother? It's Ziggy."

He groaned and stretched his legs out. "Hello, young egg. You were right about the wasps."

"Never mind that. Were you stung?"

"No, but I've got a jolly sore back."

"Let me have a look."

There was a jagged cut across his thorax. My stomach tightened.

"You have a nasty bite. Needs some honey on it. Zabel says it'll heal any wound."

"You get inside, Ziggy. I'm safe here in the long grass until I gather my strength."

"I'll be back," I said and shot into the air.

Nearing the entrance, I could see a confrontation below. A tattered guard was kicking at a wasp who was trying to get in. The little wasp jerked its head about. A large purple bruise marked its yellow face. This was the squealer from the rock wall. How dare it invade my hive? I threw myself on the wasp's back, pinning its wings back.

"Vespula rules!" it yelped.

"Did you tell her about me?"

The wasp snapped its jaws at me.

"You will suffer for your insults!" it said.

"We'll all suffer if this war keeps up," I said, losing my grip rapidly. The wasp swivelled its head until it faced me. Close up, its eyes were like polished black stones; I saw myself reflected in them. In that lull the wasp lunged and latched onto my antenna. It bit down hard. There was a jolt of pain in my head and I leaped off, releasing the beast. At that moment several guards pressed in and the wasp took off, cursing loudly.

Before it could return with reinforcements, I hurried inside the hive. Home at last. As I sat and slowed my breathing, I thought about the wasp's comment that "my insults" were to blame. Is that what this attack was all about? Zabel would know. Moving cautiously in case there were wasps inside, I made my way to the royal frame.

"Zabel, Zabel!"

"Up here, Ziggy."

There she was, near the Queen who was being groomed by her loyal attendants. The bodies of three dead wasps lay beside Zenova. Unlike the Sisters, a queen bee has the power to sting many times without harming herself. Her sting is smooth and sharp.

Zabel touched my sagging antenna and I winced in pain.

"Ziggy, you're wounded. What happened?" she asked.

"A wasp tried to eat my antenna."

"Hold still. Let me look." She dipped her foot into a cell and dabbed the honey on my broken segment.

"Yow! That stings. It looks like you had a worse fight in here," I said.

"Yes, those wasps were after babies. The Queen fought like a wildcat to protect her little ones."

Zenova approached us, followed by her attendants. Her wings were crumpled and a front leg was torn.

"What news?" she asked me.

"The entrance is secure but wasps are still targeting the honey box."

The Queen sighed. "I'll send up more defenders." She looked worn out.

"The attack is my fault," I said. "I insulted the wasps."

When I said that, I noticed the attendants whispering to each other.

"Let us be," Zenova said to the attendants. They shuffled aside, leaving Zabel and me with the Queen.

"Don't blame yourself, Ziggy," the Queen said. "I suspect Vespula sent her terror-wasps to try and make the bees afraid – not to destroy the hive. Now tell me, did you find the wild bees?"

"Yes. They're so different. Living without boxes or rules."

Zenova shook her head. "You're different too, Ziggy. That's why I've chosen you for a special job. I want you to warn another hive about the wasps. It's the green hive on the far side of the city. Their queen is very young."

I tried to picture the hive but I couldn't recall seeing it on my flight yesterday.

"After that return to me," said Zenova. "It's time I told you your family history."

"What do you mean? About when I was a baby?"

Zenova was silent. She shivered and stretched her wings. Was she wounded?

"Go quickly, Ziggy, I have orders to send." She beckoned to her attendants.

"Yes, Queen Zenova."

The attendants gathered around her again. But one of them came up to me and hissed. "You've bought this disaster on us, rulebreaker."

"Nonsense!" Zabel said. "Leave him alone." The bee turned away, head in the air.

"I tried to stop the wasps, honestly Zabel."

"Don't fret, Ziggy. Things will be back to normal soon."

She was wrong. Everything was changing. But this wasn't a good time to disagree with Zabel. What concerned me most were the Queen's words.

"What did Zenova mean about my history? You've known me all my life. You have to tell me – now."

Zabel didn't answer. She grasped one of the dead wasps with her front legs.

"Let's take this outside."

Together we carried the body towards the entrance.

"Brothers are pests," she said. "But you're not, Ziggy. You always do your best to help. I know it hasn't been easy."

"Is there something you're keeping from me?" I asked.

"I shouldn't really say. But the Queen should have told you before now. Maybe it's time you knew."

Zabel put down the wasp and looked at me.

"The truth is you don't belong with us, Ziggy. You weren't even born here. We're not your real family."

Not born here. Those three words sank into me like three heavy stones. What did they mean? I couldn't think clearly.

"But how? Why didn't you tell me before? Where was I born?"

"Slow down, Ziggy. The Queen will explain later, I'm sure. You should go to the green hive first. It's urgent."

"Yes," I said, my mind still struggling with the news. "Urgent."

"Take care," Zabel said.

I didn't reply but crawled outside, with three words dragging at my feet – not born here.

Sophie's Diary – Tuesday morning

I'm writing this while I wait for the army scientist, Captain Dawkins – he's gone to collect the bees for Project Sniffer. The army has its own hive on the farm down the road.

Something really creepy happened early this morning. I crawled out of bed and looked out the window. There was a soldier standing in the training ground. He was so still and he stared right at me. Then I realised it was only a dummy! Like something from a circus sideshow. Weird.

I have finished the book about plastic explosives. They seem pretty safe unless they are struck by lightning, which isn't likely.

The explosive looks like green plasticine – yet another nasty war toy! It hasn't got much smell but the bees should have no trouble with their acute senses.

I wish Captain Dawkins would hurry. Feeling more and more uneasy about my part in this so-called "life-saving" project. I can see rain clouds gathering outside – not very comforting.

I can't wait to get back to my own lab in the city. I'm really missing my hybrid bees.

CHAPTER 6
Humans

Back outside the hive, the fighting had calmed and most of the terror-wasps had disappeared. Everything was spinning so fast, I'd forgotten about Zeppo. I flew down to the grass. No sign. Hopefully he'd crawled inside to get first aid.

I paused for a breather. Should I go to the green hive? Why did Zenova choose me to go when I wasn't even part of the family? Or maybe that's exactly why she picked me. Then I remembered Xola. I had to find her before I did anything else.

Up at the cracked box, a lone wasp was still trying to get in. A repair team inside would be frantically sealing the gap with bee-putty, but a wild bee was pestering the wasp, making it impossible for it to settle. She flew up to join me above the hive.

"Xola, you're a welcome sight."

"Been doing some breakdancing?" she said, tapping my bent antenna.

"Ouch! Your jokes are painful. Thanks for your help out here."

"Forget it. Most of the wasps skedaddled when they realised there was no easy way in. Cowardly critters."

I told Xola about Zabel's news of my mysterious birth and my mission to the green hive.

"Fantastic, Ziggy. I knew you were more than just a bee-in-a-box."

Her reaction surprised me.

"What's so fantastic? It means I haven't got a family."

"Come on, you have a mystery to solve. Now you know you're not one of them. Hey, you might even be my cousin."

Maybe Xola was onto something. At last, I had a reason for being different.

"I suppose it explains the teasing. I really am an oddbee to them. But if I'm not a normal honey bee, then what am I?"

"Track down your family and you'll find out," Xola said.

"But where do I start looking? There must be zillions of bees in the world."

"Focus, Ziggy. Right now, you're a messenger bee. Need a bodyguard to accompany you across town to the green hive?"

"I don't think so, Xola. This is a job I should do on my own," I said. "After all, I'm Day Nine now. Besides, the sight of a wild bee will make the bees suspicious."

Xola laughed. "You're probably right. Visit my village later on, Ziggy. We need a brainy bee like you around."

"Thanks. I'd love someone to talk to. So much has happened today. Be seeing you, Xola."

Across the grassy clearing I could see the strange green hive shimmering in the heat. Would the bees there listen to an alien drone like me? Hives usually kept to themselves, except when flower workers gossiped about how strict their queen was or how much honey they'd made.

When I arrived at the entrance the guards didn't bother to challenge me. That was weird. Just inside, a team of air-conditioner bees had their backsides sticking up in the air. Water was being carried into the hive and the team fanned their wings madly over the water droplets to create cool air. I scanned the frames for an older bee to talk to but they were all newbees. The young queen must've laid hundreds of eggs.

At last, there was a huddle of older Sisters.

"I have an urgent message for your queen."

They turned and stared at me with wide eyes. It was as if I was made of wax. They returned to their circle without even a rude comment. What was wrong in here? Maybe I'd get a warmer welcome from the drones. I made my way up to the top box.

Sure enough, the Drones' Club was in the top box, although there weren't many Brothers. They were tucked into a warm corner, feeding their faces. They ignored me. I couldn't go back to that life.

Now to find the queen. I started to crawl back down the crowded frames. Too late. Sunlight flooded the hive. The roof lifted into the air and a huge shape filled my vision.

It was a head.

A human head.

I remembered the human who'd opened our hive to collect honey a few days ago. The human's hands were gentle, easing out frames without squashing a single bee. It had not even worn gloves to protect it from stings. The bees knew it was not an attack and they didn't bother the human. That was the agreement.

But now, this human was not the same. It wore a mask and gloves and it gave off an anxious smell. This was a human to avoid. It thrust a shiny tube into the top box. The tube squirted smoke into the hive. I held my breath. The dense smoke had a powerful effect on both the Brothers and Sisters. They became wobbly and many fell asleep on the spot. I fought hard to resist but eventually had to snatch in a breath. The smoke stung my lungs and my body began shutting down. If I could only crawl deeper down, before I became too drowsy.

The human began lifting frames out with its massive, clumsy hands. A bee beside me was crushed against the wall as a frame jerked past. Another bee attacked the thick gloves but its barbed stinger got stuck as it pulled away. I clung to the wax as the hand tugged at the frame I was on. There was another puff of smoke aimed directly at me and I shrank from the warm blast. The frame was lifted up and the smoke prickled my eyes and blinded me. There was a jolt and I was roughly shaken off with some other bees. We fell into a dark place.

For a time everything was still. Then we were carried a short distance and suddenly dropped. There was silence for a moment, before a new sound vibrated up through my legs. It was like the chugging sound that possums make in the night. Was this the thing the humans used to carry the honey away? Only this time it wasn't honey collection by a kindly human. This human was harvesting live bees.

The growling sound became louder beneath us. We were moving.

After some exploration, I worked out we were inside a small box. But no comb to hold onto in here, just a mass of terrified bees clinging to each other. The youngest ones were crying quietly.

"Does anyone know where we're going?" I asked.

"The humans have chosen us," said a Sister.

"Why? Has this happened before?"

"They often take bees from our hive," said the Sister.

"Where to?"

"None have returned to tell," she said.

Another bee whimpered, "Goddess save us, we're doomed."

"We're not helpless," I said. "Let's find a way out."

"Stupid drone," said the Sister, "we have no Queen to guide us now."

The bees were silent. They huddled closer together. I was on my own, again.

Right at the top of the box there was a small crack – wide enough for a hungry ant maybe, but not a bee. The world was rushing by in flashes of forest and hills. I could see that we were moving along the track at an impressive speed. Maybe I'd misjudged the humans' powers. Perhaps they were as intelligent as bees. But if they didn't want honey, what did they want from us?

I dropped to the bottom and began to think back over my day: the wild bees, the battle, and now stuck in a box again! But the thing that flipped my world was the news that I really was a different bee. The Sisters must've always suspected I was an outsider.

Who was I? Where had I come from?

Then a terrible thought came to me – what if I never found my family?

A harsh light disturbed my thoughts. The top of the box was opened a little and I could see the gloved and masked human again. Smoke billowed in through the gap, and the box was quickly tipped upside down. We were tumbled into a strange new container. It was a hard landing. This human was rough.

I'd never seen anything like this box. The walls were completely see-through. They were made from a solid unnatural material and were slippery to the touch. The other bees looked worried.

The sky had gone. We were inside now. I surveyed the surrounding room. It was rectangular, like a giant beehive box. Two humans walked slowly around us. This must be their home.

Nearby was another container with more bees huddled inside. What would they do with all these kidnapped bees? I had to find an exit, before I became a victim of the crushing hands.

At one side of the container I discovered a tunnel. But at the end of the tunnel there was a mesh wall. No way out. The timid bees were still shivering in their corner. There was no help coming from them.

The humans put their faces against the side of the box. Now I understood why the container walls were clear – they were observing us. So I examined them. One human had green material covering its entire body. Its face was a fright. It was wasp-like, with bushy black fur around the head and mouth. And what freaky eyes this human had! Ringed with dark hair, each with a single black lens in the centre.

The other human was covered in white material. Its face wasn't as scary. There was a bluish colour around its eyes, and it had shiny skin – almost like a flower. Tiny droplets of gold sparkled at the sides of its head. It reminded me of the honeydew in Xola's forest.

"Freaky" walked around the bee-box to where the tunnel was, while "Sparkles" stayed put. What were they up to? Freaky placed something in the tunnel. A sharp, acidic smell invaded the container.

I braced myself for the worst.

CHAPTER 7
Fire

The sharp smell was coming from the end of the tunnel. I crept in and saw a small blob of green putty that Freaky had pressed onto the mesh wall. It was like the bee-putty we used to plug holes at home. The bees were adjusting to the smell when Sparkles opened our lid and dropped a bowl inside. The lid was quickly shut again. The bees turned towards the bowl and began flicking their orange tongues in and out. My tongue twitched too and I was aware of an irresistible sweetness coming from the bowl. The bees swarmed over it and I was also drawn towards it.

When I reached the bowl the bees were drinking.

"Don't touch it," I shouted. "It could be a trap."

They ignored me and then I saw why.

It was sugar water, a bee's favourite junk food.

Zabel had told me that the humans fed it to bees during cold spells. I was too suspicious to drink.

Soon the bowl was empty. Then Freaky took the putty away. If this was a trick, then that green stuff was the key to it.

It happened two more times. Freaky would stick the acidic-smelling putty on the mesh, then Sparkles put in the sugar water. The bees reacted in the same way each time – their tongues flicked, then they raced for the syrup. Putty then food, putty then food.

It was easy for me to resist the stampede to drink, though I couldn't stop my tongue moving. This bunch of bees certainly didn't think for themselves.

All I had to do was figure out the connection between the food and the putty smell. Perhaps it was the scent of a precious flower that the humans were looking for. Maybe they'd release us to hunt for it. That wouldn't be so bad. But why give us the sugar water? It was like a reward, even though we hadn't done anything to deserve it.

I observed Freaky and Sparkles as they moved slowly about the room. How did they communicate with each other? Bees could send messages by dance or smell or sound. Which one did the humans use?

My concentration was interrupted when Sparkles came and peered through the walls of the container. The colourful eyes scanned the bees but then settled on me, sitting alone in the corner. I searched Sparkles's face, looking for signs of intelligence. Are you a Sister or a Brother? If only we could understand each other's language.

This human might be sending me a message now. Maybe Sparkles was saying, "I'm interested in you, Ziggy". But it would be foolish to trust these humans.

Freaky walked over and muscled in front of Sparkles and the spell was broken.

Freaky's scary hands picked up the bee-box and carried us roughly across the room. There was nothing I could do, except try to stay on my feet. We were taken outside and fresh air rushed into the box. It cleared my head after the smelly overload inside that building.

We were now in a field of brown grass. The clouds above cast a dull colour on the world. Freaky walked across the field for a short distance then put the box down. Were we being set free or was something terrible about to happen? Freaky opened the lid and ran back towards the building.

Here was a chance to escape. But it was too easy.

Why let us go after all that fuss? The huddle of bees didn't move at first. Then a sharp smell came drifting past. I pinpointed the direction of the scent. There it was – a human, standing nearby in the field. The smell was coming directly from it. The bees poked out their tongues and flew up, out of the box and towards the human. They wanted to find their sugary reward.

Now I was certain this was a trap so I waited inside the box. The mass of bees had almost reached the human. I looked at its face and shuddered.

The human had holes where its eyes should be. That wasn't the only weird thing. It stood absolutely still. This human wasn't even alive. The bees landed on its chest. The smell had signalled food and they were crawling about searching for it. But it didn't make sense because there was no bowl of sugar water out there. What was this thing with no eyes? It must be a false human.

I was about to investigate, when there was a cracking sound and a flash of light.

In that instant of brilliance, I saw the false human rip apart. It blossomed into a ball of fire, followed by a thundering wall of sound. Scorching air blasted across the top of the box. If I'd been flying at that moment, I would have been cooked.

The explosion knocked the box onto its side. And

that saved me from another terror. Glowing flakes floated down, as if pieces of the sun were peeling off. I crawled into the tunnel to escape the burning fragments. There was a strong smell in the air. Out in the field, a mushroom cloud of smoke billowed skyward. There was nothing left of the false human or the bees. Nothing but patches of flaming grass.

A layer of ash settled on the box. My mind was rattling from the blast. Was I about to die too? Apart from my aching antenna, I seemed to have no injuries.

The bees were gone. It made me sick to think of their lives cut off in a flash. I'd failed to save them. But why had the humans hurt the bees? And what was the false human?

How quickly my life had been turned upside down. Yesterday the world had welcomed me; now it was crashing in on me from all sides.

I'd saved myself from the fire but only because I'd resisted the smell. It was time to get away from these insane humans. Then I remembered the other bees still captive inside the building. There might be a chance to save them. One bee against the firepower of the humans – it was crazy.

In the distance there were more humans running

across the smoking grass. They held sticks that made loud popping sounds. They looked just like Freaky – all covered in green material.

This was my opportunity. I shook my wings and crawled out of the tunnel.

Clack! It was too late. The lid was on the container again.

Dark eyes looked down at me.

Freaky had returned.

CHAPTER 8
Hummer

I collapsed in the bottom of the box. Ziggy, the bad-luck bee – so close to freedom and now in enemy hands again. Soon Freaky would take me back inside, then the chances of escape would be zero. I'd already attracted too much attention by keeping separate from the other bees.

We'd almost reached the building when Freaky stopped abruptly and began jerking one arm in the air. What was wrong this time? Freaky dropped the box. The lid came off and I shot out like a grasshopper. I flew up and saw the cause of the upset. A dark bee was pestering Freaky – buzzing close to Freaky's head, skilfully dodging the swatting hands. Funny how a harmless little thing can terrify such a big creature, I thought. Freaky ran inside. Good riddance.

The stroppy bee flew up to join me. "You really must choose your friends more carefully," she said.

"Xola, you scared it off just in time."

"I know – I'm a perfect pest."

"How did you know I was here?"

"I saw the human arrive at Bee City, so I stayed to watch the show. Dramatic kidnapping, Ziggy. It might qualify you as a wild bee."

"Did you see the explosion?"

"Yes, it knocked me right into a web. The spider was so shocked by the blast, I had time to get free."

"It was horrible, Xola. Those poor bees, gone in an instant. But there are more trapped inside. We must save them."

She shook her head. "You're not a superbee, Ziggy. The humans have powerful weapons, and I only have a tiny sting – and my sharp wit, of course."

"What is this place anyway?" I asked.

"Come and get a bee's-eye view."

Xola led me up over the smoking field. The green humans were still chasing each other around with sticks. Beyond the field was an amazing scene – rows and rows of green buildings. I'd underestimated the humans again.

Outside the huts were hundreds of humans, exactly

like Freaky. Some were in groups, while others marched in long lines, like columns of army ants.

"You've landed smack in the middle of a nest," Xola said.

"Is this how all humans live?"

"I don't think so. These are just the fighting kind."

"It's incredible. I had no idea the humans could build as well as we do," I said.

"Just because they make fancy nests doesn't mean they're more intelligent, Ziggy."

We watched as the green humans ran around. Some carried the sticks that made crackling sounds.

"You're right about one thing – these are dangerous humans. Let's get those bees out of there," I said.

"Hold your horseflies," said Xola. "Even I'm not so reckless as to attack an entire human army alone."

"I have to try, Xola. Queen Zenova asked me to help them."

Xola thought for a moment. "It's a big problem, but I think I know where we can get some big helpers. What are we waiting for?"

Before I could ask who, she was off into the sky. I had to trust her again. I followed.

We flew back across the humans' track. The fields were on one side, the forest on the other. There was a soft mist in the air. I decided to cool off and flew through the tiny droplets of water.

Xola headed into the trees. I could hardly keep up as she zigged and zagged between the trunks like a little lunatic.

"Xola! Slow down!"

She allowed me to catch up.

"Sorry, Ziggy – you must be frazzled. But I've got a great place for you to pull yourself together."

Xola spiralled down to the forest floor and landed on a rubbishy pile. It was a massive compost heap made from layered branches. A crystal blanket covered it – raindrops shimmering on a network of spider webs.

"Welcome to Hummer," said Xola. "A haven for stressed bees. Wait here. I'll get Yogi."

Xola disappeared down a tunnel in the heap. I rested on a twig, careful to avoid stepping on a web. The last thing I needed was an agitated spider in my face.

There was a vibration through my feet. A rumbling came from within – a deep humming that reminded me of my hive. The heap seemed to be breathing.

Xola emerged from the tunnel, followed by the biggest bumblebee I'd ever seen. It had a magnificent black fur coat with wide golden bands across the back.

The bumblebee purred.

"Yogi the bumble, meet Ziggy the bee. Ziggy's had a rough day."

Yogi's voice was as deep as his fur. "Xola says you've been doing battle with the humans."

"But losing the war," I said. "They blew up some honey bees. It was horrible."

"You're safe with us, little bee," Yogi said, touching the top of my head.

I felt like crying. The bumblebee's voice was soothing.

"Tell me exactly what happened to you," Yogi said.

I poured out my story about the putty and the false human. Lastly, I pleaded for help in rescuing the bees.

"This is bad news," Yogi said. "These humans have already cut down many trees and poisoned the flowers. Now they're using bees in their war games."

"So this really is an army of humans?" I asked.

"Yes. The place you were held is a training ground."

"You mean they were training us to join their army?"

"Sort of, Ziggy," said Yogi. "The green putty is an exploding weapon. They trained you to recognise the smell of it simply by rewarding you. When the bees were released they flew straight to where the putty was hidden."

"On the false human," Xola said.

"False is right," Yogi said. "Made with human materials."

Xola snorted. "*Fmm!* Using bees to sniff out explosives. Why risk a human life when you can send bees to do your dirty work?"

"How did you learn so much about humans, Yogi?" I asked.

"It's easy for bumblebees to get inside human buildings. They think we are trapped but really we're spying on them. You should see the fuss we cause as we pretend to bumble around. Most of them kindly show us the way out."

"These humans weren't very gentle," Xola said.

"One of them was," I said. "How come you don't seem afraid of the green humans, Yogi?"

"Get to know the enemy, Ziggy, and they become less scary."

"I say we hit them hard," Xola said. "Will the bumblebees fight with us?"

Yogi squinted at her. "I think the oldbees will have a more peaceful solution. Come into Hummer and rest. We have some fine pots of nectar."

CHAPTER 9
Black Cloud

The inside of the bumblebees' nest was a wonderland. Its walls and ceiling were plastered with scraps gathered from far and wide: bark, seeds, dry leaves, and even human-made papers with curly patterns. Overhead were waxy rafters, like a gigantic rib cage. A thrumming sound echoed around the chamber.

We were given runny nectar in large wax pots. I dipped my good antenna into the drink. It tasted of forgotten flowers. Yogi left us and climbed down into a shallow pit where he joined a circle of bumblebees. They were ancient creatures with silver whiskers sprouting from their cheeks. The bumblebees hummed loudly as they discussed the problem. I could see their whole bodies vibrating.

My body ached, especially my antenna so I closed

my eyes. The thrumming sound rose and fell in one long note – *ummmm* – which seeped inside me. Xola wasn't joking when she said I'd had a rough day. I was pooped. There hadn't even been time to worry about finding my family. I had no idea where to start looking anyway.

Yogi finally came up from the pit. "The oldbees are worried about this new war game. They've agreed to ask for help from the other bumblebees in the forest."

"Thank you so much," I said. "But what chance is there against the exploding putty?"

"Weapons don't always win a war," Yogi said.

"We should hurry. They're probably training the bees now and they're a weak bunch without a queen."

"Don't be too hard on them," Yogi said. "Remember that honey bees are the *only* creature that's ever had an equal partnership with humans."

"A treaty which they've now broken," Xola said.

"Time is short," said Yogi. "First we must go to the training building. Ziggy, you lead the way."

We crawled out of Hummer and flew through the forest towards the track. I was nervous about leading, but soon found I remembered the way back without having to think about it. Like before, it was as if my brain had recorded a map of our path. The rain had stopped and the air was cold. Yogi flew slowly, floating along on his own river of air. I'd quickly warmed to this wise bee. But how strange we must look; three mismatched bees flying together.

At last, we arrived at the army nest.

"Stick with me," Yogi said.

We followed him around the building, stopping to investigate possible entry points. He flew to the roof and landed on a platform.

Yogi shook himself. "Hard work, this spying. Unfortunately, this is not like other human homes which have many entrances. There is an opening – but it could be a death trap."

He indicated a grill in the roof. I looked down between the narrow bars. Blades spun below the grill and smelly air gusted out.

"What are those spinning things?"

"The blades remove stale air from the room," Yogi said. "Like the air-conditioner bees fanning their wings in your hive."

"I may be able to squeeze through the grill," I said.

"Then what?" Xola asked. "It'll be sliced bee on the menu. Besides, you're too fat to fit."

I was miffed at her rudeness. "I'm not fat – I'm

sturdy," I said. "I can sneak between the blades if I time it right."

"But I'm the sneakiest bee here," Xola said, "so what am I waiting for?"

Without hesitating, she slipped through the grill.

Chomp, chomp, chomp went the blades. Xola clung underneath the grill. She watched the blades for a while then dropped onto the centre of the spinning circle. In a twinkling, Xola flitted between the blades. She hovered in the room below.

"I forgot to ask," Xola shouted, "what's the plan?"

"Keep an eye on the bee-box," said Yogi. "Signal us as soon as the humans pick it up."

Xola disappeared into the room.

It wasn't long before Xola called from below us.

"I think they're taking the bees outside," she said.

It was time to put the plan into action.

"Good luck, Yogi," I said.

Yogi flew off towards the forest. My job was to delay the humans. I dropped from the roof just as Freaky walked out with the container of bees. My heart sank. Freaky was covered with a mask and gloves. We should've guessed that the humans weren't going to let any pesky bees stand in the way again.

Before I could act, there was another surprise. Sparkles came out of the building behind Freaky and grabbed at the bee-box. There was a tussle between the two. What was Sparkles up to? Freaky pulled away. Whatever had been going on between them, Freaky had won the bee-box again.

Freaky walked out towards a patch of burnt grass. Another eyeless human was standing in the field.

There was no alternative now. I flew into action, buzzing as close as I dared. Freaky flicked a hand at me, but only in irritation. I flew right up and looked into the eyes. If only I could communicate with it. Freaky kept on walking. Soon it would be too late.

My tongue flickered. The smell of explosives was nearby again. We were getting close to the false human when Freaky stopped, head raised, listening to something. I heard it too – a moaning sound, like a wounded animal. The human turned and looked into the sky.

Then I saw it.

A black cloud billowing up over the roof of the building.

The cloud was alive.

CHAPTER TEN

Protest

The cloud pulsated, changing shape as it moved and making a terrific roar – the protest song of ten thousand bumblebees.

The black cloud moved across the field and formed itself into a sharp point. This cloud arrow came straight at Freaky. With a strangled cry, Freaky dropped the bee-box and ran like crazy. The bumblebee cloud stayed close behind the human who was dashing for the building. I had no idea a human's legs could go so swiftly.

I turned to the container lying in the grass. The bees were coming to their senses. I flew down to them.

"Follow me," I said. "We've got to get away before the humans return."

But the bees sniffed the air, orange tongues raised.

They'd been freshly trained. Nothing I could say would keep them from their reward.

As a mass they rose out of the box and were off.

"Stop!" I yelled. "Can't you see it's a trick?"

The bees landed on the human's chest to look for the sugar water. I flew after them. At any instant we could all be inside a fireball.

"This thing will kill you," I said. "There's no food here."

But the bees were brainwashed and continued to search.

"Scram, you stupid bees."

My eyes detected a movement from the edge of the field. Several green men ran towards us holding the sticks that smoked and banged. Soon there would be an inferno. But I'd forgotten Yogi. There was a rumble as the cloud of bumblebees hovered above us again. Yogi flew down beside me.

"You were right," Yogi said. "It's as if the honey bees are hypnotised. Fly clear, Ziggy."

I retreated to what I thought was a safe height and watched the rescue operation. The black cloud descended on the false human and covered the bees like a blanket. For a moment the bumblebees' humming became lower and a ripple passed through the swarm.

Then the cloud rose again. The honey bees had gone. The cloud lifted them and took off over the roof and towards the forest.

All at once, there was a crack and an explosion below. Flames streaked out across the field. Boiling fire raced up at me. This wasn't a safe distance at all. Luckily, the blast wave hit me first and I was carried away from the fireball. I'd never flown so fast before, riding on the turbulent air. When I was clear of the heat, I followed the bumblebee cloud into the forest.

Back at Hummer, the cloud touched down and deposited its honey bee cargo on the ground. Then the cloud evaporated. The gold-striped bees dispersed into the trees. There was no time to thank them.

Only Yogi was left.

"That was amazing," I said. "Where did you get all those bumblebees?"

"There are many bumblebees in the forest. When they heard about what the humans were doing, they joined the protest cloud."

The bewildered honey bees huddled on the ground.

"You can thank this bumble for saving you," I told them. I was about to explain the escape, when my memory was stung. "Oh, no," I said, "I forgot about Xola. She might still be inside with the humans."

"You go back for her," Yogi said. "I'll look after this lot. Fly over the treetops, Ziggy, it'll be much faster for you."

Without pausing to ask for directions, I zoomed straight up above the forest. All I could see were trees, as far as the horizon. How would I find the way? The moment that I asked the question, a picture appeared in my mind. It was another map and I realised that it showed the way to the army nest. This "mind map" was like an invisible pathway leading me along the earth below. Why hadn't Zabel told me about this skill? Did all bees have it? It was a mystery. But sure enough, Yogi was right. Without all the tree trunks to dodge, I reached the army building in half the time.

The stink of fire was still in the air. But where was Xola? Had she been captured, or hit by the chopping blades? I checked the roof first. No sign of her there so I flew around the building, but there was no way to see inside. Where on earth could I look now?

Suddenly, a human burst out of the door. It was Sparkles. I had no doubt that this human was not like the green ones. It was Sparkles who'd noticed me before and Sparkles who had tried to resist Freaky.

Sparkles walked over to a nearby building and went inside. I wanted to follow but I couldn't abandon

Xola. I shuddered to think of her hurt or captured. After circling the field and the building again, I headed slowly back to the treetops. My mind map appeared again, showing me the pathway back to Hummer. Surely Xola had found her own way back by now.

Yogi had just returned after helping the kidnapped bees find their way home.

"Any sign of Xola?" he asked.

"Nothing," I said. "Do you think she's ... hurt?"

"I'm sure she'll be just fine, Ziggy. She probably flew off to have a nectar with a friend. One of her sudden impulses."

Despite Yogi's reassurances, I stayed on edge. Xola was my best friend out here in the world. I didn't want to lose her.

Inside Hummer, Yogi and I discussed the humans.

"I can't understand why they would make the explosive weapon in the first place."

"To kill things," Yogi said.

"Then they're as bad as the wasps," I said.

I thought back to my family at the hive living so

close to the terror-wasps. My family. That didn't sound right any more. My fake family more like it. They didn't want me around. Maybe that's why Queen Zenova had sent me away.

"The whole world is against us honey bees today," I said.

"I'm not against you," said a familiar voice behind me.

"Xola! I was so worried."

"I can look after myself," she said. "I just popped home for a feed."

I shot a doubtful look at Xola. I bet she'd been off exploring. But where?

"So what's the buzz?" she asked.

"We were talking about the explosives," I said.

"Shame we can't blow up the wasps," Xola said.

Yogi gave her a stern look. "If you did that, you'd be no better than the army humans."

"Wasps deserve it," Xola shot back. "They're always making war."

"That is exactly why we must always make peace," said Yogi.

I remembered being mad enough to jump on that wasp after I saw Zeppo's body. It was hard to imagine making peace with such creatures. Who was right – Xola or Yogi?

"Well, at least you put a black cloud over their plans," Xola said.

I was relieved to hear her joking again.

"And it's time we left *you* in peace, Yogi," she said.

She was right, it was time to go. There was work to be done, like finding my real family.

We thanked Yogi and the oldbees for all they'd given us. Yogi came up to see us off.

"Take care out there, Ziggy," he said. "Our spies report a swarm of strange black bees in the area."

"Are they dangerous?"

"I just have a bad feeling about them," Yogi said.

We farewelled him and took off from Hummer. The late sun had broken through the grey at last and the air was alive with midges. Where to now? Back to the hive or search for my family? I was so exhausted I hardly knew where to turn. I found myself wishing I was tucked up safely back in the hive.

"I can't even fly straight, Xola. Can I rest in your village tonight, before I return to the hive?"

"Sure. There's an old crater you can use."

We were nearing her home when Xola stopped and dropped onto a leaf. I imitated her.

"What's wrong?" I asked.

"I want to show you something. Keep as still as you can. If you think wasps are a health hazard, then take a look at this."

Sophie's Diary – Tuesday evening

Yes! The project has failed.

First, I showed Captain Dawkins how to train the bees. It only took three training sessions for them to recognise the smell of plastic explosive – except for one cute bee that couldn't (or wouldn't) be trained. Then it was all downhill.

Captain Dawkins couldn't handle the bees. He was way too rough with them. Then the soldiers shot the test dummy and it exploded.

Those innocent bees were all killed! I felt sick.

I tried to stop the second test but Dawkins was so pushy. Then a remarkable thing happened – a bumblebee swarm appeared. Bumblebees usually only gather in natural disasters. The swarm made a sound like a giant flying chainsaw. The Captain just about wet himself.

After that, I refused to help him. He admitted that the sniffer bees were being trained for war zones. The ratbag had lied to me! I thought they would only use the bees in airport security checks – a bit like sniffer dogs. I stormed out and went back to my room.

I felt like kicking the door down. But then Dad's words came back to me, "Remember the old saying, Sophie: Anger is a stone thrown into a wasps' nest."

I was so stupid to get involved in this project.

Back to Citylab and my hybrid bees tomorrow morning. The last hybrid will be over a week old by now. Can't wait to see it.

CHAPTER ELEVEN
Revenge

Xola pointed with her antenna. A bush dripping in white flowers was in front of us. Circling the flowers was a large bee.

"Carder bee," Xola said. "That's his wife feeding on the flowers. He'll do anything to protect her. Watch."

The carder bee's partner was collecting nectar from inside the trumpet-shaped flowers. He patrolled the airspace above in slow circles. He was a chunky bee, shaped like a beetle.

Just then, a dung fly entered the carder's flight path. He pretended not to mind the fly at first and kept on moving in lazy circles. The dung fly meandered around him, but then it blundered too close to the flowers. The carder zoomed in and snatched it head-on. Before the dung fly could struggle, the carder bee sliced off its head with a single swipe. He resumed his guard patrol.

"Ouch! He makes the wasps look like ladybirds."

"He's new to the forest," Xola said. "But he's having trouble making any friends – no bee wants to go near him."

"I don't blame them, he's scary."

"Yes, he certainly is different, Ziggy."

I knew exactly what Xola meant. I was different too. And my hive didn't want to befriend me either.

We took a long detour around the bush and back to the wild bee village by the gnarled tree.

I had an underground room to myself. Sleep carried me off the second I flopped on the floor. When I woke from my nap, there was silence.

It was so quiet here – no Sisters to tease, no Brothers partying. At last, maybe I'd be able to figure out where to look for some trace of my real family. What would they look like? The same as me or something surprising? One thing was for sure, I knew I wasn't related to the carder.

That evening we sat and watched the sunlight fade from the treetops. Xola told me about fantastic forest creatures that lived in tree stumps and even under river rocks, and we drank the ultra-sweet nectar of star flowers.

She told me stories too. The one I loved most was the tale of how a human king was saved by a wild bee. The king had been challenged to find a real flower hidden among a whole palace full of paper flowers. The wild bee helped him solve the puzzle by sniffing out the real flower. I wondered if my own adventure – smelling explosives – would one day become a story told to young bees.

But I was nagged by thoughts of my hive. I still felt I was to blame for the wasp attack. If I could put that right, maybe the Sisters wouldn't hate me.

"I want to visit the wasps' nest again, Xola. Maybe Vespula will agree to a truce. It's the least I can do after all the trouble I've caused."

"Waste of time. Wasps are born bad."

"But Yogi said that it helps to get to know your enemy."

"Let me tell you a story about wasps, Ziggy. In the beginning, the Goddess created bees – but without a sting. There were plenty of flowers, life was good.

Then the world got suddenly cold and there was a terrible famine. Some bees started eating caterpillars and got a taste for flesh. The honey bees cast these meat eaters out into the wild. The outcast bees grew stings and became hunters. That's how wasps arrived in the world."

"So why do honey bees have stings now?"

"I don't know. It's only a story." Xola's voice was sharp. "The point is that wasps won't change their stripes. I'm off to sleep."

She disappeared down her tunnel. Something had annoyed her.

That night I dreamed I was back in the hive. Bees were pointing their huge orange tongues at me. Then an acidic smell flooded the hive. I snapped myself awake.

But the smell lingered – the nightmare was real. The army humans must have tracked us to the forest. The deadly putty was close by.

I crawled out to the top of the crater. The forest had just started to lighten with the dawn. No sign of the humans but they could be hiding. A breeze was blowing the smell towards me. It was coming from the old tree. I flew over and landed on a twisted root. The smell came from a dark crevice in the bark. Wedged inside the crack was a blob of green putty.

"So you located it with your keen senses," said Xola, landing beside me.

"You knew about this?"

"I found it in the army building."

So that's where she'd been yesterday.

"I'm going to get rid of those wasps – forever," she said.

"Blow them up? Then you'd be just as bad as the humans."

"Don't get all high and mighty, Ziggy. You hate the wasps too."

"Sometimes," I said. "But a war won't solve a thing."

"This weapon will end the war forever."

Xola scooped the putty out and packed it into the pouches on her legs. Why was she so fixed on destroying the wasps?

"You can't do this, Xola. It's madness – think it through." She went on packing. I tried again. "Yogi was right about you, Xola – you're just a flighty bee."

Xola ignored me. There was only one thing left to say.

"Since you won't listen, I'll have to warn the wasps you're coming."

I took off without looking back, zooming up and over the treetops. Out of the forest and along the wall I sped. I didn't know what I'd do when I arrived but I had to try.

Approaching the wasps' nest, I scanned the area. No movement below, so I landed on the top of the wall directly above the entrance. Still nothing. My heartbeat quickened as I hopped from rock to rock towards the nest. It seemed to be deserted. Or was it an ambush?

One more hop and I'd be able to see inside the mouth of the nest. A large rock formed an overhang at the entrance. There was a black tunnel below. I started creeping upside down across the surface of the overhang. My clawed feet clung to the tiny ridges in the rock. Take it slowly, I told myself.

When I was almost inside the tunnel, there was a fluttering from within, like the rustling of dry leaves.

It was such a soft sound.

Maybe a breeze blowing through the wall.

Or maybe something alive inside the nest.

CHAPTER TWELVE

Vespula

This was a turning point. I could go inside the nest or retreat to safety.

The nest was quiet again so I crept a little further into the darkness. The roof of the tunnel became difficult to grip. It was time to drop to the floor.

"Ziggy. Freeze right there." It was Xola.

She was somewhere above me on the rock.

I stopped, upside down in the tunnel.

"Whatever you do, don't move," Xola said. She came alongside and the first thing I saw was that her pouches were empty – no explosive.

"Look down there, Ziggy."

There was still nothing moving.

"See that powder on the floor of the tunnel?"

I noticed it now – specks of white dust.

"What is it?"

"Traces of human poison," Xola said. "Don't touch it – it'll kill you."

"I was about to drop onto it. It doesn't even have an odour."

"The wasps get it on their feet," said Xola. "They tramp it into the nest and before long, they're dying. The humans probably saw the wasps raiding the hives and laid poison."

"Are they all dead?"

"I'm not sure yet," she said.

Scattered in the grass I saw tiny yellow curls.

"There they are, poor little things." I actually felt sorry for the wasps.

"You're so soft-hearted, Ziggy."

"You are too, Xola," I said, pointing to her empty pouches. "You didn't bring the explosive to attack the wasps."

As I spoke the word, a shiver rippled over my body. The bristles on my face sensed a change in the air coming from the nest. There was a disturbance within. I looked into the darkness and stopped breathing.

A horror was emerging.

From the cave came an enormous wasp.

This must be Queen Vespula.

She crept into the light. Her bright yellow body tapered away to an impossibly thin waist. At the end of her striped abdomen, a sting was extended. It looked like a thorn. Her head swivelled upwards and I could see her face was covered in black splotches. Her dark oval eyes locked onto us. There was anger in them.

Why hadn't the poison killed her? How much power did she have left? Certainly enough venom to kill two little bees.

She spoke in a raspy voice. "You killed my children. Now you will die." Bubbles of foam flecked her jaws.

Maybe I could calm her down. But Xola shouted, "Go!" and took off.

I leaped into the air after her, not daring to look back.

"Get in behind," she called.

I flew close as she zoomed straight along the wall towards the forest. After a few seconds I heard a terrible sound – a fierce squealing. The enraged Queen was hurtling towards us.

The forest loomed ahead but the Queen was gaining all the time. Soon she'd be within striking distance.

Entering the forest, Xola began to weave and dodge. This slowed Vespula for a moment. But she soon adapted and began to close in again.

Vespula's squealing became more high-pitched the nearer she got. It was a sound designed to terrify her victims, to force a fatal mistake. I couldn't shut it out.

Something was wrong – Xola was slowing down, flying lower and lower. We were almost at ground level and the bushes were dense. I sure hoped Xola had a plan because any moment now the Queen would have us cornered – and my rear end was feeling exposed. Xola was flying towards a rotten old tree on the forest floor. The log was riddled with tiny holes. Brilliant! She flew into one of the tunnels at the end of the log, and I followed.

"Keep moving," she said, breathing fast.

We crawled a short distance along the narrow tunnel until we could squeeze in no further. Being smaller, Xola was able to turn around.

"We can use these grub tunnels to rest," said Xola.

Behind me, I heard Vespula's scratchy voice outside.

"Time to die!" she said.

"They love that word," I said. "But she won't reach us in here. Will she?"

There were sounds of crunching as Vespula began ripping at the soft wood.

"There's your answer. This tree is long dead. She'll easily cut her way in to us with those sharp jaws."

My heart sank. "Maybe the poison will stop her."

"It would take a lot to kill a monster like that."

We were trapped. Surely, my life could not end here, inside a rotten tree. "Sorry, Xola. I didn't think this mission through at all."

"Nonsense. I'm the one who started this wild mess."

Vespula was powering towards us through the crumbly wood. She taunted us between mouthfuls. "Feeble bees. There is no escape."

"It was the humans who poisoned your children," I called.

"Fool. I know you honey bees serve the humans," Vespula scoffed.

"No, we're partners with them," I said, but that sounded worse.

"Useless drone – you haven't even got a sting," she sneered.

Maybe she wanted an apology. "I'm sorry about all this, Vespula," I said.

"Save your breath," Xola said. "She's just trying to buy time."

It was working. Our time had almost run out.

CHAPTER THIRTEEN
The Fighters

Xola felt the tunnel wall with her antennae.

"Help me break through this wall. These passages run close together."

We started scraping and tearing at the wood. It was thin and we soon cut through to a parallel tunnel. Xola clambered through the hole.

"Time to put Plan Bee into action," she said.

Xola disappeared into the other tunnel. What was she throwing herself into now? I squeezed through the hole we'd made and followed her along the tunnel to the end. The tunnel emerged at the top of the log. I gingerly poked my head out.

There was no sign of Vespula. Here was a chance to escape while she was chewing the end of the log.

Xola had just taken off. I shook the flakes of musty wood from my wings. A sound pierced the air.

"Dieee!"

Vespula had been waiting for us. She flew up after Xola and I watched in horror.

This time there was no head start and no space to manoeuvre in the dense forest. She was trapped and there was nothing I could do to save her.

Xola was flying towards a wall of bushes covered with white flowers. The Queen was almost upon her when Xola stalled and faced her enemy. Vespula was lined up and prepared to attack.

I knew this place now. In front of the flowering bush, patrolling in lazy circles, was the carder bee. Surely the carder would spot the huge wasp. But he would see Xola too. Which one would he go for? I couldn't stand back any more so I flew up to join them.

Xola landed on a bunch of flowers right beside the carder bee's wife. Vespula homed in for the kill. There were five of us now – Xola, Vespula, the carder, his wife and me. Our lives were about to collide.

Xola tucked herself into a trumpet flower. Vespula landed on the flower and swiped at her with a spiky leg. Xola flinched and drew back into the flower. The carder bee saw the Queen wasp near his beloved partner. He threw himself onto Vespula's back. His legs gripped her thorax and she twisted to clutch at his body. The two fighters were locked together now. They toppled off the bush and plummeted to the ground.

I landed next to Xola on the flower. She was hurt.

"My leg," she groaned. "Get her away, Ziggy, before the carder comes back."

I looked down at the ground. It was a fight to the death. Vespula was bigger and flipped the carder onto his back. Maybe she would sting him now. No matter what happened, I had to protect Xola. Then I saw the carder's wife watching in shock as her partner fought the Queen wasp. Suddenly, I had a brainwave. I flew over to the carder's wife. After a quick talk, I returned to Xola.

"Don't worry about the carder," I said. "His wife has agreed to help us."

The battle below raged on. The carder flicked Vespula off. Vespula was stunned for a second, then flew head-on at the carder.

Wasp and bee collided.

One swish and off came Vespula's head.

It was over.

The Queen was dead.

The carder bee's wife flew down to join him on the ground.

"Was the carder part of Plan Bee, Xola?"

"Nah, I was just joking about having a plan. What did you say to his wife anyway?"

"I told her about the poison. I warned her that Mr Carder should wash himself immediately after touching the Queen. She was grateful. We won't have any trouble with the carder. I'm almost tempted to say thanks – he could use a friend."

"Let's go home please, Ziggy. I need to get some healer on this leg."

Back at the wild bee village, I bathed Xola's leg in nectar.

"I'm glad you decided not to bring the explosive," I said.

"I almost did. It's a good thing you were so stubborn, Ziggy. How are we going to get rid of the stuff?"

"We could mummify it."

"What are we waiting for?" Xola said.

We worked hard to seal the explosive into the tree

with bee-putty. It was a stinky job, but worth the effort as the sealer would soon harden into an airtight plug.

I smoothed off the top. "There's something I don't understand, Xola. How do you know so much about the human poison?"

"There used to be a massive wasps' nest here in the forest," she said. "It filled a whole tree trunk. The humans came one night and–"

Xola stopped. I could see she was crying.

"What happened then?"

"They poisoned the nest," Xola said softly. "But one of the wasps escaped and died in a wild bee's crater. That bee dragged the body out, not knowing she was absorbing some poison."

"Who was the bee?"

"She was my Sister," said Xola.

CHAPTER 14

Zody's Monster

We were sitting on the topmost branch of the old tree. Xola warmed her wounded leg in the morning sun and talked about her Sister for ages. She poured out stories of their adventures together when they were young.

"I do miss her, so much," she said.

"She was a Sister and a best friend by the sound of it," I said.

"Thank you, Ziggy. It's time we got your family sorted now. You need to finish solving your puzzle."

"Yes, and the biggest piece is still missing."

"Ziggy, the mystery," said Xola. "You're not a honey bee or a wild bee."

"What bee am I to be? That is the question," I said. "And where on earth will I look?"

"Yogi told me he found a whole city of humans

out there," Xola said. "Millions of them in towering hives."

"Imagine that, humans living like bees." I pictured a stack of giant bee-boxes.

"You've got a faraway look," said Xola.

"Must be time to go," I said. "I think my first step is to return to the hive and ask Queen Zenova about my birth."

We flew to the rock wall. Here I was, on the edge again, just like my first flight. My world was a lot larger now. I knew that I could survive beyond the hive. And I had made friends out here.

"Good luck with your search, Ziggy. You know I'm here if you need me."

"Thanks, Xola. You look after that leg."

"I won't let it out of my sight," she said.

I smiled. "Goodbye, friend."

I flew along the wall towards my hive, maybe for the last time. I tried to picture my real family. Would I have hundreds of Brothers and Sisters? What would the Queen be like? I'd find out the truth about myself when I got back to the hive. The more I thought about it, the more I suspected that Queen Zenova had been guiding me all the time. She'd sent me into the forest first, and then to the green hive. It was as if she wanted to push me far beyond Bee City to find something – or someone.

The clearing was ahead and the hive came into view. I flew straight to the top box and there was Zabel in her favourite spot, waxing her legs. Nothing had changed.

"Don't you do any work?" I said, landing next to her.

"Ziggy, you're alive!"

"Of course. A little cooked around the wings, but still kicking."

"There was a rumour the humans took you. But I knew you'd survive," she said.

"Zabel, I've so much to tell you. But first I need to see the Queen."

"I'm sorry, Ziggy, but the Sisters don't really want you back in the hive."

So they still blamed me for the wasp attack. "But the Queen is the only one who knows about my family," I said. "She's the link to my future."

"You're too late, Ziggy. I'm afraid Zenova is dying."

I remembered her injury from the wasp attack.

"Dying? But she can't die. What will happen to the hive?"

"A new Queen has been chosen – she's about to hatch."

My last hope of finding out the truth was almost gone. "Do you know where I'm from, Zabel? Please think."

"I didn't want to be the one to tell you this, but here goes."

I tried to get ready for more bad news.

"I remember the day when you arrived as a baby," Zabel said. "Queen Zenova asked me to keep an eye on you. She said you were a special bee and I had to protect you while you were little."

"Why can't I recall that day?" I asked.

"Because you were sound asleep. A human smoked the hive and then placed you in here."

This was the next piece of the puzzle – a human had delivered me to the hive!

"But why? Can you describe the human?"

Before Zabel could answer, a Sister appeared at the edge of the box.

"The new Queen's hatching," said the Sister. "Come quickly."

"Gotta go, Ziggy. It's my duty."

When the Sister heard my name, she glared at me.

"Fly away, Oddbee."

Zabel had flown down to the entrance. This was my last chance. I took off. I dived off the edge and hovered above just as she was walking inside the nursery.

"Zabel!" I yelled. "What did the human look like?"

She turned her head to me and called out. "Like a fl–" but I couldn't hear the last word because at that moment, a hairy guard bee buzzed right in front of me.

"Move along, boyo," it said.

This was not my home any more. In that second I decided I had to leave and that I could never go back. I shot into the sky and watched as the hive got smaller and smaller below me. I turned over the fragment of Zabel's last words in my brain. A human like a ... what was she trying to say?

Where to now? No other hive would accept me: the rule was "stick to your own". The humans' track rolled off into the distance in front of me. It led to the army base – my least favourite place on earth. Yet the answers lay with the humans. I was finally free of the hive but that meant I had to choose my own direction. There was no queen or friends to guide me.

I started flying along the track. One of Sister Zody's warning stories replayed in my head: "When I was young I saw something nasty on the track – a monster that sucked up bees and squished them under its black paws."

Thanks for that cheerful story, Zody.

But I had to risk it. I flew higher to get a view of the

track ahead. Maybe I could find that human. If I could only get to the city. The moment I thought about the city, a mind map popped into my head. This time it was a pathway stretching to the horizon on the earth below. Was this the way to the city? But how could I know the way if I'd never been there before? I knew I had to trust this strange map if I wanted to find my family.

As I flew, I remembered Zenova's words, "You are different." She knew where I'd come from. Maybe she'd been trying to point me in the direction of the humans.

The mind map guided me for a short distance over the track then turned off on a side branch. It was there that I spotted the first "shell". The object was moving along the track. It was shaped a bit like a huge snail's shell and I dropped down to get a closer look. The shell thing was growling as it moved. I knew that sound. This was a human means of transport.

I flew alongside it and could see a human sitting inside. The shell was quite fast but it wasn't hard to keep up with. The track hugged the contours of the land which meant that the shell had to turn many corners – while I simply flew in a straight line over the hilltops.

My mind map was still strong. Gradually, the human track became wider and busier with more and more shells joining it. Curiosity about these clever humans led me down to investigate again. Now I saw that not all of the travelling things were shell-shaped. There were very thin ones that looked like the back end of an earwig. The biggest were giant boxes that acted as if they owned the track.

I was looking at a group of small humans sitting inside a shell, when one of the huge boxes came roaring alongside me. Stinking smoke gushed out. As it passed by, it sucked all the air towards it and I tumbled out of control.

This must be Zody's monster!

I tried to fly up but I was pulled towards its spinning black paws.

CHAPTER 15
City of Humans

The smoky air carried me right underneath the giant box. Just as the spinning paws were almost upon me, I was flicked out the other side of the beast, riding on the current of rushing air. I ended up in the long grass.

I rested for a few minutes on a wide leaf. I was shaking and my bent antenna throbbed. There was a droplet of water on the leaf and I took a cool drink. It seemed like the world was against me. I couldn't let it keep me down though – I was alone and nobody else was going to pick me up.

I focused on the human city again. I flew back up over the track, but this time when the monster boxes came speeding past I kept my distance.

Now there were hundreds of travelling shells moving

like a rapid river. The land itself began to disappear: fields gave way to more and more buildings. Was this the beginning of the human city? Soon there were so many buildings that I could hardly see a patch of green or a tree.

My mind map was fading fast. I scanned for landmarks but everything looked the same: rows and rows of identical buildings and tracks crisscrossing between them. To make it worse, the air over the city was laced with fine dust and my breathing became wheezy. Suddenly, the mind map ended. Gone. Worry turned to panic.

Beneath me was a large building – the last point on my map. I flew down to it. The structure was quite different to the army buildings. There were many openings in the walls and I could see humans inside. There were five levels, like the towers at Bee City. I decided to explore each layer, starting at the top of the building.

I hadn't got far when a bee flew past me. It was a drone with large eyes and a mop of fuzz on his head.

What was he doing here in the middle of the city?

"Good morning," he said. "Coming in?"

The bee flew straight at the wall and disappeared. I moved closer and saw a tiny circular tube. Should I follow? Was it another trap? But what else could I do? I couldn't go back now. I flew in through the hole.

Into the humans' world.

The tube was made of the same slippery material as the army containers. I crawled through and emerged into the weirdest beehive I'd seen – if it was a beehive. It only had two frames of wax comb and the walls were see-through. But where were all the bees? There should be thousands.

I looked into the room where a human was standing with its back to me. The human turned and looked through the wall, directly at me. I stared back and could hardly believe it. There were the honeydew sparkles, the colourful blue eyes – like a flower. It was Sparkles!

"Welcome to Open Hive," said the bee, who'd invited me in. "My name's Wiri." He extended an antenna.

"Ziggy," I replied, touching the tip of his antenna with my good antenna.

"We don't get visitors here," said Wiri. "Most bees avoid Open Hive. They can't stand the bright light in here. Do you know why you are here, Ziggy?"

The bee's question was strange and I was uncertain how much I should reveal about myself.

"I'm looking for some old family members." That was true at least. "Where are all the other bees? And why is Sparkles here?" I asked, regretting using my pet name for the human.

Wiri laughed. "Sparkles! We call her Teacher. You seem pretty chummy with her."

So Sparkles was a Sister human, not a Brother. I looked up into her face again, but at that moment she turned and walked to the other end of the room.

"I named her that because of the honeydew on her head."

Wiri smiled at me. "Do you know who you are, Ziggy?"

"I wish I knew," I said. "I've been asking myself that question for some time. I'm a lost bee looking for his family."

"I'll tell you who you are," he said. "You come from a hive far from the human city. All your life you were teased by your Sisters, while you never felt at home with your lazy Brothers."

This was bizarre. He knew me! My stomach knotted. Was this another trick? I had to be sure.

"Not bad," I said. "But any intelligent bee could have guessed those details. Of course a lost honey bee would be rejected by a hive."

Wiri went on. "Your queen sent you into the world so you could develop survival skills. Finally, you found out that a human had placed you in the hive as a baby and you went looking for your family."

I was gobsmacked. It'd taken me a lifetime to unravel my story – Wiri had done it in seconds.

"It's all true," I said. "How did you work it out so quickly?"

"Simple. The same thing happened to me and to all the bees in Open Hive."

"You were all put out into hives by the humans?"

"Just by one human – Sparkles. Has it clicked yet, Ziggy?"

Sparkles was my human! *Like a flower.* That's what Zabel had been trying to say.

"Do you know why you ended up here?"

"Something guided me," I said. "An invisible map. I call it a mind map."

"Which means that a part of you must have known the way," Wiri said.

Now it started to make sense. I knew how to fly to Sparkles's home because I'd been here before.

"Do you know who I am, Ziggy?"

I looked closely at Wiri – the silky hair, the bulging eyes and solid body. He was so familiar all of a sudden.

"I'm your Brother," said Wiri. "You were born here."

"You're my Brother?" I repeated. The words were like the sweetest honey. I felt the knot in my stomach dissolving. Had I really found my family?

"I know you'll want more proof," said Wiri. "First you should meet the rest of the team."

As he spoke, the "team" were entering the hive through the tube. I counted five bees.

"How did the mission go, Florian?" asked Wiri.

The biggest bee spoke. "It's worse than we thought. The killers are already in the city."

"Did you find their nest?"

"Sister Osmia has a clue about that," Florian said. "Are you going to introduce us to our new Brother?"

"My great pleasure," said Wiri. "Ziggy, meet your family. Your Sisters, Osmia, Calluna and Tilly. And your Brothers, Florian and Barnum."

One by one they touched my antenna and welcomed me. They looked at me so fondly. It was too good to be true but here they were touching me – my family. At last, I was home.

Florian stepped forward. "We've been expecting you, Ziggy. You must have a million questions."

He wasn't kidding. I tried to speak but felt all choked

up. I swallowed and turned to Wiri. My Brother. I could hardly wait to say it aloud.

Wiri touched me with his front leg.

"I cried a whole day when I got home," Wiri said.

"Tell me everything, Brother," I said.

Sophie's Diary – Wednesday

The most wonderful thing has happened – I've found the seventh hybrid bee! Or I should say that he found me.

I drove back to Citylab this morning. When I got there, I saw the bee in the hive. He must have used the planet's magnetic field to find the way back home. His magnetic sense must be very highly developed.

This is definitely the hybrid bee I planted in the farm hive. And he has a bent antenna, just like the cute bee I saw in the army lab. If it's the same one, he's a real survivor, explosions and all.

He's now housed in the lab hive with the other hybrids.

I'm making good progress in my efforts to decode their language. These bees may be much more intelligent than I imagined. I've been teaching the first hybrid simple signals which he is beginning to understand.

Unfortunately, while I was away with the army, there was another bee attack in the city. A group of guys was poking a bee swarm and one young man was killed. I suspect they are aggressive Africanised bees. Sadly, it's attacks like this that make people scared of all bees. The sooner we find them the better. But where do you look in a city of a million people?

CHAPTER 16
Impossible Mission

"We aren't true honey bees," said Wiri. "I suppose 'human' bees might be a better name. We each started life in the same way: the Teacher – Sparkles – created us here in this building. See that door?" He pointed at a black rectangle in one wall. "She keeps the queens in there.

"After we hatched, Sparkles placed us in hives around the city, where we were raised. But your hive was out in the countryside, far away. We each followed our map home, but we wondered if you'd ever make it back. You must be a brilliant navigator."

"So you mean I'm not the only one with a mind map?" I said.

"We all have one. The Earth is full of energy. We can see the energy pathways below as we fly over the ground."

"Why does Sparkles do all this?"

"She works with bees all day – it's her job."

"So why did she create us?"

"Because we're more advanced than other honey bees," Wiri said. "You must have known you were different, Ziggy."

"Oh yes, I was told that every day of my life. I was the rulebreaker, never happy to go along with the crowd, always questioning."

"None of us fitted in either. But you'll feel at home here, Ziggy. We're a new kind of bee – each with a special ability."

"Superbees," I said.

Xola would have laughed at that.

Wiri smiled. "We help Teacher with her tests and experiments and she feeds us in return."

I wondered if my special ability was my mind map. Maybe that's why Sparkles put me in a distant hive. She'd been testing me.

"At the moment we are on the verge of a crisis in the city," Wiri said. "The killers are on the move."

I suppose I should've been shocked by all Wiri had said, but I was loving it. Just being here and talking to my real Brother was all I wanted right now.

Wiri led me to the top of a frame where the other

bees were in a circle. I was aware of Sparkles moving around the room beyond.

Florian greeted me. "Welcome, Ziggy," he said. A bronze-coloured bee, Florian seemed to be the oldest in the family. "Let me update you. A swarm of killer bees has entered the city. These black bees are very dangerous."

I wondered if these were the bees Yogi had warned me about.

"They've already attacked a human who provoked them. If they start invading beehives, it will be a disaster. Over to you, Osmia."

Sister Osmia was a young bee with a long body and orange fur above her eyes. "The killer bees can't stand cold," she said. "So I've been visiting some warmer buildings. I spotted some bees hanging around the Sick Home – it has vents where they could be hiding."

"What's a Sick Home?" I asked.

"It's where they take humans for treatment," Osmia said.

"Well done, Osmia," said Florian. "Our mission is to locate the killers' nest and figure out a way to trap them. Seven bees against a thousand."

"Impossible odds," Wiri said. "I like that."

"Speed is essential. We must reach them before the swarm spreads," Florian said. "We'll fly to the Sick Home and split up there."

"Can I come too?" I whispered to Wiri.

"We're counting on it," he said. "Your skills will be needed."

What skills did he mean? I wasn't sure I wanted to be tested again.

The group moved down the frame and I followed them towards the exit tube. Then a shadow fell across us. I looked up and there was Sparkles looking down. It was only then that I realised there was no roof on the hive. She reached in and I backed away from her hand. But the others didn't move.

Sparkles touched Florian gently on the back.

"What's she doing?" I asked Wiri.

"She's going to track our movements."

Sparkles attached a shiny disc to Florian's back. It had an antenna sticking out of it. He made a low buzzing sound and then circled three times.

"I knew humans were intelligent," I said, "but this is amazing. Is Florian trying to communicate with her?"

"He's been teaching her simple signals. She's learning fast."

"What does the antenna do?"

"It sends out a signal to follow. Pretty basic."

"Let's go, team," Florian said.

We trooped out through the tube and flew away from the building. I looked back and saw Sparkles still watching us. How I longed to discover the human language for myself so I could talk to her.

We headed towards a cluster of towering buildings in the city. There was so much movement everywhere. Below us, I saw crowds of humans on the ground and many more of the shells speeding past. We flew in a beeline until we got close to an ugly building made of grey stone.

"The Sick Home?" I asked.

"That's right, Ziggy," said Wiri. "The stone even looks sick."

Wiri's jokes reminded me of Xola.

As we hovered above the building, Florian spoke to us. "Wiri, you take Ziggy and Osmia to check out the bottom. The rest of us will start at the roof. Look for nesting places. Meet you at the middle."

The three of us dived down the sheer side of the building. Wiri led the way. He plummeted like a hawk towards the ground – faster than anybee I'd ever seen. I struggled to keep up.

We joined him at the door to the Sick Home. There were many humans coming and going. I'd never seen them in such large numbers, and such funny shapes and colours. One was even being pulled along by a dog!

"You're a fast flyer, Wiri," I said.

"It's my special skill – watch."

He zoomed off and caught up with the dog and its human. The dog was panting madly, its slobbery tongue hanging out. Wiri circled its head, then suddenly flew right inside its mouth and out again before it could react. The startled dog snapped at the air.

"Wiri's the impulsive one," Osmia said.

"I've got a wild bee friend just like him."

Wiri returned, a big grin on his face.

"You'll be a dog's dinner one day," Osmia said.

Wiri laughed. "Let's start circling."

We flew in slow orbits around the Sick Home, gradually moving up the building. There were openings in the wall through which I saw humans. This really was a human hive and I wished Xola was here to see it.

"Why all the fuss about the killer bees?" I asked Osmia as we flew.

"The humans can't stop them spreading. They're deadly for bees too. If a single killer bee gets into a hive, it infects the honey bees with its violent nature. Gentle bees are transformed into war-like bees overnight."

"Nasty," I said. "We'd become like the wasps."

About halfway up the building, it happened. I was flying in a straight line when I was jerked off course. It was as if something reached out and grabbed me and I found myself heading towards the stone wall. Before I could correct my flight path, I bounced off the wall and hit something hard. What hidden menace had I stumbled upon this time?

CHAPTER 17
The Deadly Bees

For a moment I was stunned by the impact. When the fogginess cleared, I saw that I was on a narrow ledge.

"Are you all right?" It was Osmia, landing beside me.

"No damage," I said. "Something zapped me. There was a burst of energy from inside the building, I think. It's stopped now."

"I felt it too," she said, "but it bowled you over."

"It's the same feeling as my mind map," I said, "but a hundred times stronger."

"You seem attracted to energy, Ziggy," said Wiri, hovering overhead. "Maybe that's your gift. Can you fly now?"

"Hang on. Maybe we should find the source of the energy burst," Osmia said.

"I dunno," Wiri said. "Finding the killers is more urgent."

"Trust me on this," Osmia said. "It may be useful."

"Okay," said Wiri. "But we must hurry. I'll go in through a stink room and check it out."

Wiri flew into a pipe sticking out of the wall. An awful smell came from within.

"A room for humans' droppings," Osmia told me.

I tried desperately not to imagine that.

"What's your special ability, Osmia?" I asked.

"I haven't discovered it yet."

"Does that worry you?" I said.

"No – I'll recognise it when the time is right. And the family don't make a fuss about it."

Wiri emerged from the pipe.

"Did you find anything?" I asked.

"Your senses were bang on, Ziggy. There's a human invention behind that wall. It might be creating the energy bursts. Barnum will know."

"Here come the others now," Osmia said.

The rest of the team flew down to meet us on the ledge.

"Tilly has spied the swarm with her sharp eyes," Florian said. "It's round the back. How did you three get on?"

Wiri told them how I had found the energy source.

"Excellent work, Ziggy," said Florian. I glowed in his praise.

"Barnum is our expert on the humans," Florian said. "Any ideas?"

The smallest bee in the family stepped forward. He was almost completely hairless, like a little worm.

"The humans use this invention to heal their sick," he said. "It releases a powerful blast of Earth-energy. You must be very sensitive to it, Ziggy."

"No wonder he's a great navigator," Wiri said.

I hardly knew where to look – I'd never had so much praise before. It felt good.

"I have a plan," Barnum said. "We can use this invention against the killers."

Barnum told us his idea. It was dangerous but the team was so confident that I was completely caught up in it. Florian had the tracking antenna so he was to stay behind on the ledge on the side of the Sick Home and wait for Sparkles. The rest of us were to fly around to the back to meet the killers.

When we arrived at the rear of the building, we looked down towards the pipes. Rising steam obscured the view.

"I can see the swarm," Tilly said. "They're attached to a grill above those pipes. They aren't moving."

I looked harder. There it was – a black sphere clinging to the wall. This mass of bees could corrupt hives everywhere if it escaped. Honey bees would then turn on the humans and there would be war.

"There's an opening into a room above the swarm," Tilly said.

"We want to spend as little time in the Sick House as possible," Wiri said. "Stick together team, we've got a killer date."

We followed Wiri as he dived towards the pipes.

As we got nearer, I could see that the bees were stirring. The killer bees were awake.

I glanced down as we passed the swarm. The killer bees were much smaller creatures than I'd imagined – about half my size. They were black and shiny. The surface of the swarm quivered as our shadow brushed it. We'd been noticed. Hopefully they weren't interested in a few stray bees.

We flew quickly in through an opening above them. Inside the room there was a human lying down, but with one leg raised in the air. The leg was covered in a solid white case. It looked like a moth's cocoon. Wiri led the charge. We flew at the human's face and landed on its skin and in its hair. A gurgling sound came from its throat.

I felt sorry for the human. It thought we were going

to hurt it. The weak creature started shaking and droplets of sweat formed on its head. This was exactly what Barnum had predicted. As the beads of sweat trickled down the face, we crawled through them and smeared the salty water all over us. I was surprised to find it had a pleasant taste.

The human was now shivering madly. It reached out and touched something that made a buzzing sound. A few moments later another human entered the room. It sprang forward when it saw us.

"Let's skedaddle," said Wiri.

We flew back towards the window. The human lay in torrents of sweat, but seemed pleased to be free of our attention. Its fear was now clinging to our bodies – and that was the idea. We exited the room just as the opening was slammed shut behind us.

Now for stage two of Barnum's plan. We hovered over the killer bee swarm and began to flick our wings. The human sweat splattered all over the black bees below. The swarm began to convulse and it let out a sound like a bird screeching.

"Go!" Wiri shouted and we shot away, tracking the wall of the building. Behind us, the swarm ripped itself from the grill. It flew after us in a tight ball formation.

Barnum had told us that killer bees get angry extremely quickly. They also hate the smell of human sweat. It's an instant alarm and a signal to attack. We'd drenched them in sweat – so they had good reason to be upset.

We flew mighty close to the wall, dodging pipes and ledges as we went. The killer swarm could barely keep up with us. There were so many obstacles for a mass of bees and they weren't especially fast flyers. We rounded the front corner of the building and I hoped that Florian was ready for us. If Sparkles wasn't there yet, we were in big trouble. Where do you put a swarm of killer bees while you wait?

At last, we were back at the ledge. But Florian had disappeared. I glanced behind and saw the black bees coming around the final corner. Soon they would be upon us in an unstoppable stinging frenzy. I looked into the room. There was an opening in the wall so we flew inside. Sparkles was standing there beside a huge tunnel.

"Quick everyone, down here," Florian called. He was on the floor below the mouth of the tunnel. I wasn't sure what would happen next, but I trusted my older Brother completely. "Prepare for a shock," he said.

As we dropped to the floor, the swarm arrived at the window. It paused, then flew in for the kill. The air was filled with the sound of a thousand angry wings. But something was wrong. It wasn't us the killers were after now. They sensed a much better target. The killers headed straight for Sparkles.

Everything happened at once. In an instant I was pinned to the floor by a massive burst of energy. My body felt like it was being crushed. Even my Brothers and Sisters struggled to keep on their feet. There was a powerful force coming from the strange tunnel above us.

Just as the killer bee swarm reached Sparkles, it was struck by the blast of energy. The mass of bees flipped in midair and began to rotate – slowly at first, then faster and faster. The ball of spinning bees was pulled towards the tunnel. I could hardly take a breath, the energy had drained me so much.

The swarm became a tornado of bees and it was being dragged into the tunnel by the force field. Finally, the whole swarm was suspended inside the tunnel. Sparkles slammed the tunnel door to seal them in.

Then the energy stopped and the weight lifted from my body.

"Yes! We did it," Wiri said. "Let's have a look at the nasties."

We flew up and looked into the tunnel. The swarm

had collapsed inside. The killer bees lay in a tangled heap, unable to fly or walk.

"That was cutting it close," Florian said. "Well done, team."

"Let's hope there are no more swarms in the city," Osmia said. "At least Sparkles knows how to trap them now."

"What's in that tunnel?" I asked.

"It's a clever invention," Barnum said. "It can concentrate the Earth-energy into one spot. Works well on a big ball of bees."

Exhausted, we flew back to Open Hive and had a large feed of honey. It had been the longest – and best – day of my whole life. I'd joined in a dangerous mission and I had discovered my special gift – to be able to sense the energy of the Earth itself. But most wonderful of all was discovering my real family. I couldn't wait to get to know them.

Sophie's Diary – Thursday

A breakthrough with the hybrids. I placed a radar transmitter on the first hybrid and tracked him to the public hospital. The signal led me to the MRI scanner room.

I saw the hybrid bee sitting outside the window so I let him inside. I wondered if his flight was disrupted by the scanner. The huge magnet inside it is thousands of times stronger than the Earth's magnetic field.

Then the other hybrids arrived, followed by a large swarm of bees. I recognised them at once – the rogue Africanised bees.

The swarm flew at me and I froze. Time stood still and I thought of Dad. But I had the perfect weapon. I switched on the MRI and the swarm was sucked inside the scanner.

It was incredible. My hybrids had not only found the Africanised bees but had led them here. Some would say it was a coincidence. But I know that honey bees are at the top of their branch of the tree of evolution – and this proves it.

Tomorrow I'll take the seventh hybrid up to the abandoned hives. Maybe I can find out what's causing the bees to disappear. Peter's doing a helicopter delivery up to a farm so we'll hitch a ride with him.

CHAPTER 18

In Shock

I spent the next morning talking to Sister Osmia. She gave me a tour of Sparkles's room first. There were boxes with coloured lights everywhere, rows of see-through containers and inventions that only Barnum could explain. The thing I loved most was a square of paper. On it was a picture of Sparkles and a smaller human. Was this her child? Did that mean she was a human queen?

Osmia described the tests that Sparkles gave them: recognising shapes, solving mazes, even smell training. When I told Osmia about my own smelly adventure with the human army, she was angry.

"It makes me sick. I'm afraid you can't trust all humans."

"I thought the army humans hated us," I said. "Except Sparkles. She seemed different."

"I love the way you call her that," Osmia said. "There are still some things we don't understand about Sparkles," Osmia said. "Like that door in the corner."

The black door revealed nothing – no crack to crawl under and no light from within.

"The special queens are taken in there. Sparkles gets them from all over the world."

Poor Queen Zenova came to mind and a wave of sadness passed over me. She'd been so kind to me and so brave. I told Osmia about the terror-wasps.

"No wonder that wasp you bruised was annoyed – wasps are precious about their face markings."

"The Sisters still blame me for the attack on the hive," I said.

"At least you made an effort to put things right."

While we'd been talking, Sparkles had entered the room. She came over to the hive and looked down at us. Her large hand hovered over me, but this time I didn't try to escape. Sparkles placed a small box right beside me.

"Looks like you've been chosen for the next mission, Ziggy," said Osmia.

"Surely she doesn't expect me to go alone."

"It's up to you," Osmia said.

"Will you come with me?" I asked.

"Sure, Ziggy. I love it when Sparkles goes flying."

I smiled but I didn't really get her joke.

We hopped into the box. It had breathing holes in the sides and we could see out.

"I hate boxes," I said. "They always seem to lead to trouble."

"Wait till you see the dragonfly," Osmia said.

"I've never seen one. Zody called them the ugly bugs."

Sparkles carried us to the roof of the building. Osmia had not been joking. There was a dragonfly waiting for us – only this was a giant one. It had long wings on top and a large bubble-like eye in the front. There was a human sitting inside the eye.

The wings started to spin. *Flack, flack, flack.* They went around faster and faster. Sparkles climbed inside, still holding us in the box.

"The humans like their noisy inventions, don't they?" I said.

"It's not just a noise-maker," Osmia said, grinning.

Then to my astonishment the dragonfly lifted into the air.

"We're flying!" I said. "But hang on – humans can't fly."

"Not by themselves," she said. "They have to use a copy of a dragonfly. Enjoy the ride."

The flight was a little slow compared to bee travel but it was more relaxing. We could look at the land below and talk at the same time. The dragonfly took us beyond the city, across flat farmland, then over ranges of scrubby hills.

"Who's the other human?" I asked.

"He takes Sparkles out to visit hives," Osmia said. "He controls the dragonfly."

So this was a Brother human as Freaky had been. He had stubbly whiskers on his face and dark, shiny coverings over his eyes.

"I'll call him Beetle."

Osmia laughed. "When I was growing up in a hive, they called me Twiggy because I'm thin."

"Don't worry. I was once called Fat Boy."

"That makes us fatty and skinny," she said.

After flying over endless brown hills, we finally dropped into a steep-sided valley. I began to feel queasy, looking out through the holes in the box.

The dragonfly touched down in a meadow between a rocky riverbed and some trees. Sparkles picked up our box, climbed out of the dragonfly and walked towards the trees. Beetle stayed inside. Soon, the *flack-flacking* blades spun faster again and the dragonfly lifted off. It disappeared over a ridge, leaving us in the valley. Now the only sound was water roaring over rocks.

"I wonder why she brought us here?" I asked Osmia.

"I think she wants us to explore the area."

Sparkles put our box on the ground and opened it. I felt woozy.

"Can bees get airsick? Because I'm feeling crook," I said.

"You just need some fresh air," Osmia said.

Osmia flew out and I followed her. I'd barely got above grass level when I suddenly felt my stomach turning over. As I looked up at the surrounding hills, the feeling only got stronger. I tried to land again. But I couldn't. Instead, I found myself flying upside down and heading in the opposite direction up into the sky.

With a huge effort, I focused on Sparkles and brought my wings under control. I was still flying upside down but I managed to circle Sparkles before landing in the dirt at her feet.

Osmia settled beside me. "Cool trick. Trying to impress Sparkles, eh?"

"No way. My flight controls have flipped – don't know what's wrong with me."

"It's not you, Ziggy. There's something wrong with this valley. Look over there."

There was a cluster of beehives under the trees but no sign of any bees.

"It's a sunny day – there should be hundreds out harvesting."

"Deserted hives are spooky," I said.

"There are no butterflies or bugs here either," said Osmia. "It's as if all the life has been sucked out of the valley."

"Not quite," I said. "There's a creature coming this way."

It was a lone bee, hopping from flower to flower. But it didn't even look up at us.

"Hello," Osmia called. "Where's your family?"

"It's the end," said the bee, her face still inside a flower.

"The end of what?" I asked.

The bee leaped out of the flower and flew at my face. She stopped and hovered eye-to-eye with me.

"The world!" she yelled. "It's the end of the world!"

"Calm down," I said. "We won't hurt you."

The bee suddenly grabbed me with her front legs and shook my head about. "They're gone!" she shouted. "She took them all." She let me go and flitted off to bury her head in a flower again.

"She's crazy," I said.

"In shock more likely," Osmia said. "Something must have frightened the other bees off."

I thought of all the terrors I'd met in the last three days: wasps, army humans, killer bees.

What monster had driven everything from this valley?

"I saw some more hives across the river," Osmia said. "I'll have a closer look."

"I'm not going to be much use with my wonky flying," I said.

"Don't worry," Osmia said. "I'll stay close to Sparkles."

But I was determined not to miss out. "Let me try again."

I lifted off but was quickly flipped over again. This time I kept my eyes on the ground and used it as a guide. The trick worked as long as the ground was mostly flat.

"I think I could get used to this topsy-turvy view,"

I called to Osmia. "I'm quite good at upside down flying."

"Don't let it go to your head, Ziggy."

I got that joke.

Osmia led the way down to the river. Sparkles had to run to keep up with us. It wasn't bad being upside down as long as I kept a fix on the ground level. We reached the river and Osmia crossed first. But when I passed over the rushing water, I lost my focus. There was nothing level to fix on and I got too close to the river. It only took a split second for a spray of water to hit my wings and I was blasted out of the air.

CHAPTER 19
Sting

I aimed for a green rock in the middle of the river and landed with a splat. What a mess this was – everything was going wrong. I'd have to dry my soggy wings fast before the river swept me away. I began to shake the water off while trying to avoid the constant splashes over the rock. Osmia probably hadn't even seen me fall. I looked back and saw Sparkles step into the river. Who was she following?

"Let me help, Ziggy." Osmia landed beside me. She fanned her wings at me.

At that moment, Sparkles hopped onto a slimy boulder and her legs flew out from under her. To my horror, she hit the water with an almighty splash.

"Never mind me, Osmia. Sparkles is hurt." I shook off the last drops.

Osmia flew across and I struggled after her, still flying upside down. We found Sparkles lying across a large rock, her lower body under the water.

"She's still breathing," Osmia said, hovering above her head. "Maybe she's knocked out."

"Will she wake up?" I asked.

"If the water doesn't reach her first. Humans can drown just as fast as bees."

The river tugged at Sparkles's legs. It was impossible for us to move her to safety. If only Yogi's swarm of bumblebees was here, it could lift her out. I looked at Sparkles's face. All the colour had drained out of it and one of her sparkles was missing. There was just a tiny hole where it had been.

Don't leave us, Sparkles. But what could I do?

"Maybe Queen Vespula was right, I am a useless drone."

"Ziggy, you genius!" yelled Osmia. "You're a drone – but I'm not. There is one way we could wake Sparkles."

She flew onto Sparkles's hand and began tapping the skin with her stinger. I realised what she was going to do and dropped onto Sparkles's arm.

"Stop, Osmia! You'll die if you sting a human."

"It's the only way, Ziggy. We can't let Sparkles die."

She was right but I couldn't let Osmia die either. My Sister.

"Please, Osmia. Zabel told me that the sting gets stuck. You'll bleed to death."

"I've made up my mind, Ziggy. I'm sorry."

I had to think fast if I was to save both Osmia and Sparkles. What did I know about stingers? They have tiny hooks so they'd easily get stuck in tough human skin.

"Wait!" I said. "If you're going to sting her, come up the arm a bit. The skin is softer there. There's a chance you won't get stuck."

Osmia landed next to me and raised her sharp stinger. She plunged it into Sparkles's arm. The venom flowed from Osmia's body into Sparkles.

Nothing happened for a moment. Then Sparkles's arm twitched violently, throwing us both off. I flew up but Osmia dropped onto the stones below.

I landed beside her.

"You're still alive!"

"And Sparkles?" she whispered.

"The pain is working," I said. Sparkles was groaning and rubbing her arm. "Let's get out."

"Can't move – no energy," Osmia said.

Sparkles rolled over towards us and nearly squashed us. I grabbed Osmia's leg and took off.

We were clear but I was losing my grip on Osmia. I headed for the riverbank using all my strength. At least her weight kept me upright.

We came down with a crash, landing in the soft grass. It took Osmia some time before she could talk.

"How do you feel, Queen Osmia?" I asked.

"What do you mean?"

"Well, only a queen bee could sting and survive."

"I'm no queen, Ziggy."

"Maybe this is your gift, Osmia. The power to sting more than once."

"It could be or it might have been the soft skin. Either way, I won't be trying it again in a hurry."

"For emergency use only," I said.

While we rested, Sparkles came out of the river and walked slowly back to the deserted hives. She flopped under the tree and we joined her. After a while we heard the dragonfly returning to the valley. I couldn't wait to escape this deadly place.

Back at Open Hive we recovered with some honey and told the others about our adventure. I thought Florian would be disappointed with us for failing our mission but he was just pleased to see us home safe. Barnum had an idea about why the sick valley had upset my flight. He said something might be buried there that made the Earth-energy act strangely. Everyone agreed that Osmia's stinging ability was the best skill yet because she'd saved Sparkles's life.

"I think we need a picnic after all that excitement," Florian said.

We flew out of the city for the rest of the day. Florian asked me to lead. I proudly guided them over the forests. One day I'd take them to visit my old friends – but not now. This was family time.

I did miss the others: dear Zabel had risked a lot by taking an outsider under her wing and Xola had taught me so much. But it hadn't been easy for me in the hive. Now I understood why. A beehive had to be highly organised and bees must follow orders. But a bee like me didn't belong in a box. I needed to be free to think and explore.

I turned in a new direction and spotted a pond. Then I saw it – a blue patch below. The blue heaven. My family followed me down to the flowers. We feasted in the sun.

Sister Calluna praised my choice of flowers. She knew all about flowers, their scents, pollens and even ones that could kill a bee. As we lay in the grass, Barnum told me about a human invention that could fly higher than any bird. Those crazy wingless humans!

I loved my new family. Each one had a special strength, which I guess was why Sparkles had assembled the team.

"This nectar is the sweetest thing," Osmia said.

"You've chosen well, Ziggy," Florian said. "We'll need all our wits for the next mission with Sparkles."

I smiled at his use of Sparkles's name. It had caught on.

"What mission? Where to?" I asked.

"I think it's going to be a long trip this time. Far across the world."

I hovered and looked down on my Brothers and Sisters flitting from flower to flower. I looked at the blue above and the blue below.

I remembered Zabel telling me once, "You can't change things, Ziggy". But now I had a place in the world. I couldn't wait to see where Sparkles took us next. The adventure was just beginning.

Maybe I could change the world – even without a sting.

Sophie's Diary – Friday

Yes, I was stupid – again. I shouldn't have gone out alone but it was worth it in the end. I released the bees in the valley and the seventh hybrid did something truly amazing – he flew upside down!

At first I didn't know why. I tried to track him across the river but I slipped on a boulder. I ended up lying stunned, half in the water, my back so sore I didn't dare move – then to top it off, one of the bees stung me! This wasn't my lucky day. Lost one of my gold earrings too.

I sent a text to Peter and he kindly came back early and choppered us home. Fortunately no broken bones, just embarrassment.

It was only later that I realised why the hybrid was flipped upside down. He's sensitive to magnetic fields, of course. This means the magnetic field beneath the entire valley has reversed. The magnetic poles of the planet flip every 250 000 years. This valley could be the start of a magnetic flip that will spread to the whole planet. At least we will be prepared for it now – and all thanks to one small honey bee. He'd be the perfect bee for the Aurora satellite.

It also occurred to me that the bee that stung me may have been trying to help. Bees that care about humans? My fellow scientists would never believe that, but Dad would have. Just before he died, he said to me, "The only way humans will survive, Sophie, is to learn to see the world through the eyes of the smallest creatures."

Dr Sophie Domisse's Guide to Bees

Bees are my Life – and Yours!

We scientists are fascinated by bees. Maybe that's why bees are one of the most studied creatures on Earth – and because humans would not survive without bees. Bees pollinate flowers which then make seeds and fruit. Without bees, we wouldn't have many fruits, vegetables and even meats.

But my favourite gift of the bee is honey. Bees get nectar from flowers then turn it into honey in the hive. They're the only insect that makes food we eat. Honey bees harvest an amazing two million flowers to give us a half a kilogram jar of honey. You even get different flavours of honey from different flowers. I like heather honey best. Scientists have proved that honey has healing power – it actually fights bacteria.

Meet the Bees

Believe it or not, over 22 000 kinds of bee have been discovered.

Honey bees: These are the bees that have interested humans all through history. They are very social bees, living together in hives. A hive has one queen, about 40 000 working females and 300 lazy male drones.

Wild (or Native) bees: These small bees live in their own private burrows. Some of them leave soil piled at the entrances, like tiny volcanoes. Wild bees are not aggressive and help pollinate many plants.

Bumblebees: Okay, they are big and noisy, but I can tell you they're peaceful bees. They rarely use their stingers. They don't make honey but keep nectar in wax pots.

Carder bees: These ones attack other insects a lot.

Killer (Africanised) bees: One of the most violent species. A scientist in Brazil created them by crossing bees from Africa and Europe. But 26 killer queens escaped from his lab and they're now spreading through the Americas, invading beehives. They attack much faster than other bees.

Hybrid bees: These bees are bred in labs by scientists who cross different bee types to produce bees with distinct abilities.

Wasps: Believe it or not, these pests are in the same insect family as bees. Wasps have jaws so they can eat insects (and baby bees). They are able to recognise each other's face markings. They also raid honey from beehives.

Bee Wolves (or Bee-killer Wasps): These are wasps that catch honey bees on flowers. They paralyse them and take them back to a nest. There, they lay eggs in the living bees. The bee-wolf larvae eat the bees.

Incredible Honey Bees

Bees have some amazing abilities. Humans like to think we're the only ones using a language of symbols (writing), but there's one other creature that does – honey bees (surprise!) They use a special dance to tell other bees where the best flowers are found.

They're great navigators too as they are able to make a kind of mental map to guide them. Bees can also tell the time because they have a body clock like ours. They sleep at night, but do bees dream?

We've discovered that bees are intelligent. They can learn and solve problems. They can also be trained using sugar as a reward and will quickly create a lifetime memory.

Even though honey bees live for just over a month, they have very full lives. Bees are always changing jobs. A bee starts life as a cleaner – then becomes a babysitter, a builder, then a chef, a security guard and an undertaker. Later it goes outside as a food collector and scout.

Charles Darwin described the comb of the hive bee as perfect. And it is! The wax honeycomb is one of the lightest, strongest, least wasteful structures known. Bees build the six-sided cells to store honey, pollen and babies.

They even have an air-conditioning system. It is very clever. The bees cover the comb in water and fan it. I have seen a beehive near a lava field (temperature 60 °C!) where the bees kept the hive cool inside.

The queen is the boss of all the hive activity. She uses smell chemicals to keep her huge family well behaved in the hive.

Are you scared of bees? Don't be. Honey bees won't sting you if you leave them alone. They only sting in defence because they will die after stinging a human or large animal. Their barbed stinger gets stuck in tough skin and they bleed to death. I'm more nervous around wasps – they can sting you over and over without dying.

Bee Senses

You have five senses. Bees have six!

Sight: Bee eyes have thousands of lenses (a human eye has one). Bees have three extra eyes on top of the head. Bees can't see the colour red but love blue flowers.

Smell: Bees use their antennae to smell. Their sense of smell is 100 times more sensitive than ours.

Taste: Bees taste with their antennae, tongues, and through their feet! This means a bee only has to touch a flower with its front feet to decide if it's tasty enough.

Touch: Bees' antennae are very sensitive. Their bodies are covered in tiny hairs that can feel changes in the air to help judge wind speed and direction.

Hearing: Bees don't have ears but they can hear through their legs and antennae. However, they can't hear human voices clearly.

Magnetic: Most impressive of all, bees have magnetite crystals in their body to sense the Earth's magnetic field when flying.

The Vanishing Bees

> ***"From London to Los Angeles, from Slovenia to Taiwan, honey bees are dying. Scientists grapple for answers to perhaps the deadliest and certainly the most costly bee epidemic ever to hit the planet..."***
>
> Alison Benjamin and Brian McCallum,
> *A World Without Bees*

Help! In recent years billions of honey bees have disappeared all across the planet. The cause is a mystery. Is it disease, pesticides, climate change or all of these?

Life on Earth really does depend on a small insect. In other words, if the bees disappear, then so do we. Without bees, there would be no apples, no carrots, no pumpkins, no cherries or strawberries (please, not that!), no nuts or avocado. No more dairy products, beef or bacon either – because bees pollinate the plants that we feed to cattle. Without bees, wild animals and plants would die out.

How can we save the bees?

There are lots of things we can do:

- Use less toxic chemicals on plants.
- Reduce pollution of the air and waterways.
- Plant lots of flowers and trees.
- Remember that bees are our partners in life. Honey bees are not farmed animals. We have a one-of-a-kind deal with them: a safe home in exchange for all their work.

Spelling Bee

beehive = home for bees, made by stacking boxes in a tower

bee-putty (*propolis*) = a sticky material for repairs in the hive

cell = hexagonal storage holes in the wax comb

dance = a bee's dance steps spell out information about flowers: the direction, distance and even the quality of the nectar

frames = wooden rectangles (like picture frames) which sit side by side in bee-boxes. Bees build wax comb on the frames

honeydew = sweet liquid excreted by tiny insects.

Humans eat it too!

pollen baskets = pouches just below a bee's "knees"

Author's Note

When I was 12 years old, playing alone in the garden, a swarm of bees flew over me. I thought the world was ending and ran inside. Then a few years ago someone gave me the strangest Christmas present – a beehive. As I learned about bees, I realised they weren't aggressive and I started to enjoy their company in my garden.

I got the idea for *Sting* after reading a newspaper report that told how the army had trained bees to sniff out explosives in war zones. It made me angry to think of bees involved in human wars. Then I heard about the mysterious disappearance of bees worldwide – and I knew I had to imagine the world through a bee's eyes.

At the beginning of the story Ziggy is eight days old in bee time. He'd be about 12 years old if he was a human boy. Much of the bee behaviour in this book is true. (Okay, I know bees don't speak English!)

Visit my website for more bee science, stories, poems and puzzles:
www.raymondhuber.co.nz

Acknowledgements

A huge thank you to all those who encouraged my writing, especially my wife Penelope Todd, Emma Neale who helped me to shape *Sting* and Virginia Grant who did a superb editing job. Thank you also to Professor Alison Mercer, Dr Kyle Beggs and the Bee Team at Otago University for their wonderful bee science. And *Sting* wouldn't exist without the gift of a beehive from Fiona and Ione Todd.

For permission to quote their brilliant books, thank you to:

Alison Benjamin and Brian McCallum,
A World Without Bees,
Guardian Books, 2008

Hattie Ellis,
Sweetness and Light: The Mysterious History of the Honey Bee,
Hodder and Stoughton Ltd, 2004.

WANTIRNA COLLEGE
Harold St. Wantirna
Victoria, Australia 3152
Ph: 9801 9700 Fax: 9800 2590
email: wantirna.sc@edumail.vic.gov.au